011

REKI KAWAHARA　ABEC　BEE-PEE

SWORD ART ONLINE
Alicization turning

SWORD ART ONLINE

"Um, we made it ourselves, so I hope you like it."

Tiese § The trainee page attending Eugeo as he strives to become an Integrity Knight.

"Kirito, if you're that comfortable around them, you don't need to keep running away anymore!"

Eugeo § The first resident of this world whom Kirito met. A fellow elite disciple of Kirito's at the North Centoria Imperial Swordcraft Academy.

"Ah, quite good.
In fact, Ronie and
Tiese, I might go so
far as to say that this
is the equal of the
Jumping Deer."

Kirito § A boy who found himself within a mysterious fantasy realm. He seeks the system console that will allow him to escape.

"Wow, really?!"

Ronie § The trainee page attending Kirito as he strives to become an Integrity Knight.

"Urgh…hrg…aaah…! I—I…!"

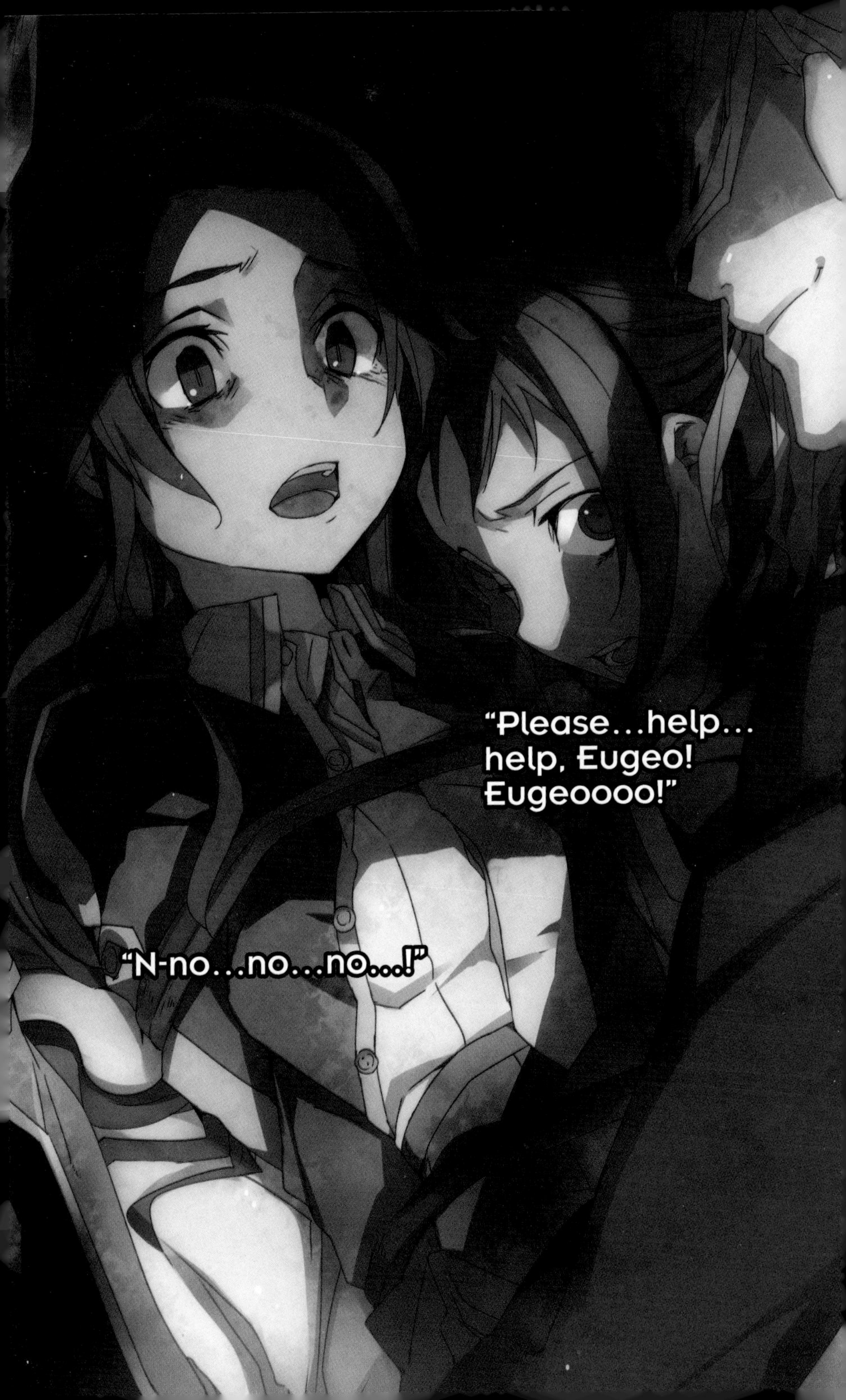
"Please...help...
help, Eugeo!
Eugeoooo!"
"N-no...no...no...!"

"Axiom Church of Centoria, Integrity Knight—
Alice Synthesis Thirty."

Alice § An Integrity Knight tasked with keeping
order in the human world.

The North Centoria Imperial Swordcraft Academy and the Integrity Knights

Within the Underworld, Centoria is the capital city, located directly in the center of the human realm. Over 20,000 citizens reside within its perfectly circular walls, encompassing a diameter of ten kilors. Within that circle, barriers known as Everlasting Walls split the city into four parts in an unusual X-shaped configuration. The four quadrants are called North Centoria, East Centoria, South Centoria, and West Centoria, and they serve as the capitals of the four empires that preside over the vast human realm.

At the very center of the city is the Axiom Church's massive, white Central Cathedral tower. Its pinnacle is so high that it can barely be seen, and looming walls hide the square grounds of the church from sight. It is from this cathedral that the Everlasting Walls splitting the city spread outward. The Axiom Church is the overriding organization presiding over all of humanity. Its military officials known as Integrity Knights are tasked with maintaining order and serve as inspiration to the training swordfighters, who look up to them.

In order to enroll at the North Centoria Imperial Swordcraft Academy and continue along the path to becoming an Integrity Knight, students must first pass the entrance exam and become primary trainees. Trainees work hard from dawn to dusk for an entire year, then take an advancement test to reach the next level. All students strive to qualify for the Imperial Battle Tournament, but Kirito and Eugeo want to be glorious Integrity Knights, which necessitates winning the Four-Empire Unification Tournament, the very highest competition of swordsmanship in the human empire.

Map Illustration: Tatsuya Kurusu

SWORD ART ONLINE

Alicization turning

VOLUME 11

Reki Kawahara

abec

bee-pee

SWORD ART ONLINE, Volume 11: ALICIZATION TURNING
REKI KAWAHARA

Translation by Stephen Paul
Cover art by abec

This book is a work of fiction. Names, characters, places, and incidents are the product of the author's imagination or are used fictitiously. Any resemblance to actual events, locales, or persons, living or dead, is coincidental.

SWORD ART ONLINE
©REKI KAWAHARA 2012
All rights reserved.
Edited by ASCII MEDIA WORKS
First published in Japan in 2012 by KADOKAWA CORPORATION, Tokyo.
English translation rights arranged with KADOKAWA CORPORATION, Tokyo, through Tuttle-Mori Agency, Inc., Tokyo.

English translation © 2017 by Yen Press, LLC

Yen On
1290 Avenue of the Americas
New York, NY 10104

Visit us at yenpress.com
facebook.com/yenpress
twitter.com/yenpress
yenpress.tumblr.com
instagram.com/yenpress

First Yen On Edition: August 2017

Yen On is an imprint of Yen Press, LLC.
The Yen On name and logo are trademarks of Yen Press, LLC.

Library of Congress Cataloging-in-Publication Data
Names: Kawahara, Reki, author. | Abec, 1985– illustrator. | Paul, Stephen
   (Translator) translator.
Title: Sword art online. Volume 11, Alicization turning / Reki Kawahara,
   abec ; translation, Stephen Paul.
Other titles: Alicization turning
Description: First Yen On edition. | New York, NY : Yen On, 2017. | Series:
   Sword art online ; 11
Identifiers: LCCN 2014001175 | ISBN 9780316371247 (v. 1 : pbk.) | ISBN 9780316376815
   (v. 2 : pbk.) | ISBN 9780316296427 (v. 3 : pbk.) | ISBN 9780316296434 (v. 4 : pbk.)
   | ISBN 9780316296441 (v. 5 : pbk.) | ISBN 9780316296458 (v. 6 : pbk.) | ISBN
   9780316390408 (v. 7 : pbk.) | ISBN 9780316390415 (v. 8 : pbk.) | ISBN 9780316390422
   (v. 9 : pbk.) | ISBN 9780316390439 (v. 10 : pbk.) | ISBN 9780316390446 (v. 11 : pbk.)
Subjects: | CYAC: Science fiction. | BISAC: FICTION / Science Fiction / Adventure.
Classification: pz7.K1755Ain 2014 | DDC [Fic]—dc23
LC record available at https://lccn.loc.gov/2014001175

ISBNs: 978-0-316-39044-6 (paperback)
       978-0-316-56103-7 (ebook)

10 9 8 7 6 5 4 3 2 1

LSC-C

Printed in the United States of America

"THIS MIGHT BE A GAME, BUT IT'S NOT SOMETHING YOU PLAY."

—Akihiko Kayaba, *Sword Art Online* programmer

SWORD ART ONLINE

Alicization turning

Reki Kawahara

abec

bee-pee

CHAPTER FIVE

1

The Underworld.

That was the name of the world, but because it was in the sacred tongue and not the common language, hardly any of the world's residents understood its meaning.

At the center of the Underworld was the human empire, a realm encompassing a circle 1,500 kilors across. A rocky range called the End Mountains formed its border. Beyond that was the Dark Territory, home to nonhuman races like goblins and orcs—or so it was said. Almost no humans had ever seen it for themselves.

The human realm was split into four empires, the northernmost of which was the Norlangarth Empire, a place of fertile fields, deep forests, and numerous lakes. At the southern tip of the fan-shaped empire was the capital of North Centoria. The other three empires were structured exactly the same way so that the four capitals connected to form one small circle, the entirety of which was simply called "Centoria."

At the dead center of Centoria was the towering stronghold of the Axiom Church that formed the center of the world, ruling over the four empires with its unbreakable Taboo Index and Integrity Knights that together upheld the structure of the realm.

The tower was known as Central Cathedral, and it seemed to

stretch nearly all the way to glowing Solus above. It was the center of humanity in all respects—which meant that it had to be the center of the Underworld as a whole, as well.

This was the world as Eugeo knew it.

Two years had passed since the spring when he'd left his little village of Rulid—at the far northern reach of the northern empire—with his partner, Kirito. They had made their way into the sentinel garrison at Zakkaria, largest town in the north, and then left for Centoria last spring with a handwritten recommendation from the garrison commander. There, they cleared the entrance test for the North Centoria Imperial Swordcraft Academy, the empire's finest school for swordfighting; worked hard for a year as primary trainees; and scored two of the top twelve spots on the advancement test.

Rather than becoming secondary trainees, those twelve high-scoring students were granted the title of "elite disciple." Disciples got their own dorm building with a roomy training hall, freedom from many of the onerous regulations of the academy, and an entire year of intensive training to prepare for their next goal: an appearance in the Imperial Battle Tournament.

The daily studies, sword instruction, and free training time were exhausting, but it was a dream come true for Eugeo. If he hadn't met the peculiar black-haired Kirito in the forest two years ago, he would still be swinging his woodcutter's ax until the day he retired of old age. Instead, he was mingling with the children of Centorian nobles, learning sword techniques and sacred arts, and making progress toward his true goal.

Unlike the other pupils, Eugeo's dream was not merely to triumph in the gloried Four-Empire Unification Tournament and ascend to be one of the few, proud Integrity Knights. He wanted to be a knight so that he could pass through the gate of the Central Cathedral—a privilege even first-rank nobles did not possess—and reunite with Alice Zuberg, his childhood friend who had been taken there years ago.

This infinitesimally small hope had lain dormant for years

until Kirito had come along and rekindled it. In fact, the two had worked together to overcome every obstacle blocking their path. Eugeo helped teach Kirito the Basic Imperial Laws that he'd lost all memory of, and Kirito taught Eugeo his unique Aincrad style of swordfighting. They'd come this far by acting like brothers... like twins.

Even now, as elite disciples, Eugeo and Kirito shared lodging in the dormitory. But they shared only the common space, as each had his own bedroom. While Eugeo still felt guilty about the beds being far bigger and softer than any back home in Rulid, their bathing room having as much hot water as they wanted, and their ample portions at the elite disciples' mess hall, Kirito had adjusted to all of it almost instantly.

Even Kirito, though, had at least as much trouble as Eugeo at one particular thing.

The dormitory was not the only privilege the top twelve received from the academy. Every disciple had a primary trainee who served as his or her page and personal servant. Eugeo himself had been a page to an open-minded and generous disciple last year, and he'd actually enjoyed it quite a bit...but things were different once the tables were turned.

Eugeo's page was a sixth-rank noble girl named Tiese Schtrinen who had only just turned sixteen. Kirito's page was another sixth-rank girl of sixteen years named Ronie Arabel, and these two were a source of severe discomfort for two boys from the countryside.

For her part, Tiese didn't seem bothered by the relationship at all. The lively girl with burning-red hair and reddish eyes of a tint rarely seen in the far north was blessed with plenty of motivation and dedication, and as her tutor, Eugeo often felt that he was the one getting lessons. But the part he would never get used to was having his needs attended to by a noble, three years younger than he and a *girl* to boot. Every single day, he would complain that he could take care of some task or another, and Tiese would insist, "No, this is the page's duty!"

Kirito's situation with Ronie was similar in many ways. Over the past month, whenever she'd showed up to clean his room, he'd often managed to find some reason not to be there.

On this, the seventeenth day of the fifth month of the year 380 HE, Kirito waltzed back into the room just as Tiese and Ronie were done cleaning. He had a large paper sack in his arms, full of the delectable honey pies from the Jumping Deer over on East Third Street in North Centoria District Six. He removed one each for himself and Eugeo, then gave the rest to the girls and instructed them to share with their roommates.

Primary trainees were forbidden to leave on weekdays, so of course they could never go out to market to buy treats like this. The girls were ecstatic at this unexpected gift, and it was the first time Eugeo ever saw them run, rather than walk, back to the primary trainee dorm.

Part of the disciple's duty was to bond with the page and teach them in all areas of life, not just swordfighting, so perhaps the foodstuffs were a part of that effort—but Eugeo couldn't help but find it more like simple bribery. He glanced sidelong at Kirito, who finished chewing his pie with a satisfied grin and said, "So, Eugeo, shall we engage in a little practice before dinner?"

"I don't mind in the least, but remember, tomorrow's the higher sacred arts exam. And it's not just a written test but a demonstration of your least favorite subject: generating ice elements."

"Ugh…"

Kirito had been reaching for his wooden practice sword, but this reminder stopped him short. He seemed to be grappling with his impulses for several seconds, then sighed and lowered his hand. "Why do I still have to study for tests after coming this far…?" he muttered wistfully.

As Kirito said, Eugeo never imagined himself studying sacred arts in Centoria when he was a simple woodcutter in Rulid. Sword practice was, of course, much more fun than memorizing complex rituals, but if they neglected their sacred arts studies, eventually even top marks in swordsmanship would not be enough to win them entry into the Battle Tournament.

Of course, Kirito didn't need Eugeo to explain any of this to him. He swept back the black hair that matched his uniform and said weakly, "Eugeo, I'll be studying all the way until lights-out, so if you could bring my supper from the mess hall, I would appreciate it."

"Got it. You know, you'd find it a lot easier if you just studied it bit by bit on a regular basis."

"You are indeed correct, young Eugeo. Alas, not all of us are capable of such feats," Kirito lamented, plodding across the living room. He soon vanished through the north door into his bedroom.

Unlike the primary trainee dorm, the elite disciples' quarters were totally circular. The building's three-story structure was hollow inside, with interior walkways lining the walls, and the bedrooms were all located along the south exterior.

On the first floor were the mess hall and shared bath chamber, while six student rooms made up the second floor and another six occupied the third. Each pair of rooms had a shared common room between them, and Eugeo and Kirito's suite was on the third floor.

Room placement was determined automatically by the individual results of the end-of-year exams. The top scorer received Room 301 at the east end of the third floor, second place got Room 302, and so on, such that the twelfth-place student was in Room 206 on the second floor. Eugeo was in Room 305 and Kirito was in 306, which meant that out of the 120 primary trainees, Eugeo had ranked fifth overall and Kirito sixth.

Their adjacent ranks were partially a result of intent and partially just good luck. Originally their plan was for numbers one and two, of course—that being the only surefire way to get paired together—but in the practical test against the sword instructors, Kirito scored fourth and Eugeo fifth. That would have split them apart, but Kirito lost points in the exhibition of forms and sacred arts, which bumped him down to sixth.

So they achieved their goal of sharing a common room, but it also created a new concern.

In one year—no, ten months—they needed to graduate as first and second in the class so they could qualify for the Imperial Battle Tournament. Kirito had been seventh and Eugeo eighth on the school entrance exams, so this was an improvement, but it was hard to be optimistic with four others ranking above them.

Kirito seemed to be more relaxed about it, as if just being an elite disciple was his only goal. His confidence wasn't without merit. Disciples' ranks were determined by test matches held four times in the year, rather than the overall scores from the previous year. These matches were against other students, not instructors, so rather than using traditional scoring criteria, winning was all that mattered.

And Eugeo's norms-busting partner, as a primary trainee just two and a half months ago, had defeated the former first-seat disciple in a one-on-one duel. Technically, the judge ruled that it was a draw, but given the circumstances, it was undoubtedly a victory for Kirito. His foe was the son of a second-rank noble house that traditionally served as sword instructors for the Imperial Knights.

Eugeo had his own confidence in his abilities thanks to two years of instruction in Kirito's own Aincrad style. But he wasn't as optimistic as his partner. He certainly wasn't cocky enough to ignore his daily regimen, even the night before a written test when book study was crucial.

With his sparring partner withdrawing to his room for an emergency cram session, Eugeo had no choice but to take his own sword and leave.

Beyond the interior hallway across from the door was the hollow space from the ground all the way up to the skylight cap on the roof, through which the red of the sunset was visible. There hadn't been a building this extravagant even in Zakkaria, much less his humble home of Rulid. The floor beneath his feet was luxurious, polished wood, and the curved interior wall featured several works of art based on imperial history.

If I told my brothers back home that I lived in such luxury and even had my own servant, they'd never believe me, he thought as he made his way down the long walkway.

Elite disciple or not, he was still just a student getting VIP treatment. If this was what he got *now*, what kind of lifestyle comforts must the mighty finalists of the Unification Tournament receive—to say nothing of the Integrity Knights ranked above any of the four emperors?

"...Whoops!" he said, rapping his head with the wooden sword resting on his shoulder.

After a year at the school, Eugeo was getting used to it, but there were times that he felt guilty, as if he'd forgotten how he'd felt when he'd left home. He was here to raise his profile as a swordsman, not to indulge in the comforts of wealth and fame.

"Alice," he mumbled, reminding himself.

Everything he was doing here—winning the test matches, striving to be an Integrity Knight—was merely a means, not the goal. It was all to gain access to the Central Cathedral, so that he could be reunited with his childhood friend imprisoned inside it...

He descended the stairs on the northern side of the building and headed for the special training hall adjacent to the dorm. This was another privilege of the disciples—as a primary trainee, he'd practiced the sword at the packed hall and outdoor training grounds, but now he had a spacious area available at any time, with no waiting period.

At the end of a short walkway, Eugeo pushed open the door and was greeted by the fresh scent of the training hall floorboards, which were replaced every spring. He stopped, started to breathe in a fragrant lungful, then froze. There was an oily, clinging perfume mingling in the air.

After he proceeded through the changing room into the hall, his foreboding was confirmed.

Two male students in the center of the wood floor noticed Eugeo and scowled. They were practicing their forms. One of them had paused with his wooden sword held aloft, while the other was adjusting the angle of his feet. Both of them lowered their arms in a very pointed way.

Don't worry, I'm not going to steal your forms, Eugeo thought. He gave them a brief bow and headed for the corner of the training hall. He figured they would ignore him like usual, but this time, one of them stepped toward him and said, "Well, well. All alone tonight, Disciple...*Eugeo*?"

It was the one who'd been raising his sword. His broad chest was wrapped in a vivid red uniform, and waves of golden hair flowed down his back. There was a pleasant smile on his handsome face, but the way he had paused before saying Eugeo's name and lingered on it after was a subtle dig at Eugeo's birth to a frontier family that didn't have its own surname.

Responding to each and every minor slight would be a waste of good training time, so Eugeo ignored the barb and replied, "Good evening, Disciple Antinous. Unfortunately, my room partner—"

The second man cut him off with a screech. "Insolence! When you speak Raios's name, you must address him as 'First Seat Disciple'!"

This one had gray hair tamped down with oils and a pale-yellow uniform. Eugeo turned to him with more open distaste and bowed. "Please forgive me, Disciple Zizek."

The other man bristled even more and stomped forward. "You commit insolence upon insolence! You must address me as 'Second Seat'! You betray the rich history and tradition of our hallowed academy with every act..."

"Now, now, Humbert," said the first man, clapping his partner on the shoulder.

The fellow with the gray hair, Humbert Zizek, was indeed the second seat of the twelve elite disciples, while his golden-haired partner, Raios Antinous, was the first seat—the man who had taken over the position from Volo Levantein, whom Kirito beat in a duel before the end of the school year.

Unlike Volo, who had the quiet air of an accomplished warrior, Raios exhibited a higher noble's opulent arrogance—yet their sword styles were quite similar. That had a lot to do with the fact that they both practiced the High-Norkia style, but it was still strange. Raios was refined (and twisted), while Volo placed all his focus into one straightforward, overpowering attack.

When Eugeo had mentioned this to Kirito, the other boy had said that half the skill of noble children came from the tremendous self-esteem instilled into them for years. In terms of dedication to his craft and training, Raios couldn't hold a candle to Volo, but his sense of self-worth (or arrogance) was far greater, and that was how his blade could have such a nasty, insistent weight.

"But isn't self-esteem supposed to be basically the same thing as pride? If they have so much pride, why do they stoop to petty pranks?" Eugeo had wondered.

Kirito had thought it over and replied, "Pride is something that you have to continually prove to yourself. But self-esteem doesn't work that way. Raios and Humbert shaped their identities by comparing themselves to others. So at each and every opportunity, they feel the need to keep us inferior, because we're not even from Centoria, much less of noble birth. They can't maintain their sense of self-importance otherwise."

Eugeo found this difficult to understand, but if Kirito was correct, that meant willfully submitting to their arrogance only fed their self-image and strengthened their skill with the sword.

That suggested the option of returning their aggressive insults with his own, but unlike Kirito, Eugeo didn't have the keen ability to toe the line when it came to school rules, and he didn't want to sow the seeds of conflict for no good reason.

And so, feeling slightly ashamed of his passive nature, Eugeo simply bowed to indicate his apology, then headed for the corner of the training hall again. As he walked across the unfinished boards, pristine and freshly cut from a nearby forest, Eugeo's foreboding slowly eased. With all the stone buildings in Centoria, the scent of fresh wood was a precious source of peace.

Raios and Humbert might have had personal instructors since they were children, but for seven years in Rulid, I hit that Gigas Cedar two thousand times a day. I might not have their level of self-esteem, but I certainly have pride. Even if I was only swinging an ax, not a sword...

He stopped in front of one of the logs standing along the west wall for personal practice. These had been replaced at the same time as the floorboards, so the sides were hardly dented at all. Eugeo gripped the platinum oak practice sword with both hands, held it at default mid-level, and focused his breathing.

"Sha!"

He lifted the sword over his head, then brought it down with a quick cry. It smacked heavily against the right side of the thirty-cen-wide log, which trembled to its core.

Eugeo took a step back, savoring the vibration in his wrists, then swung down on the left side. Then right, then left. After ten strikes, his mind drifted from his body and sword, leaving nothing but the block of wood.

Eugeo's nightly practice consisted of four hundred of these alternating high strikes. He did not practice the complex forms from class that Raios and Humbert had been performing just now. Kirito was his sword style master, and he said they weren't necessary.

In this world, what you put into your sword is crucial, Kirito liked to say when he was teaching Eugeo. *The High-Norkia, Baltio, and Aincrad styles' secret techniques are very powerful. Once you have the knack of how to activate them, the sword practically moves on its own. The problem is what comes next: Like you saw with Volo and me, you're going to have more clashes of ultimate attack versus ultimate attack. Once it comes to that, the weight of the sword will determine the outcome of the fight.*

Weight.

Eugeo understood that he wasn't simply referring to the physical weight of the swords themselves.

To Volo Levantein, the pride in his birth to the clan of the traditional instructors of the Imperial Knights gave weight to his sword. For Golgorosso Balto, whom Eugeo had served as page last year, it was the physical perfection of his body. For Kirito's tutor, Sortiliena Serlut, it was the polished bite of her attacks. And for Raios and Humbert, it was the respect of their noble birth.

So what do I put into my sword?

When Eugeo had asked this, Kirito smirked and replied that it was his job to figure that out. But then he realized that this wasn't a very good example for a teacher and added that Eugeo wouldn't find it by practicing his forms.

So all along their journey to Centoria, and even after they made it to the academy, Eugeo continued practicing his strikes nearly every day. He wasn't a noble by birth or a swordsman—all he had was years of practice repeating those simple ax strikes in the forest near Rulid.

But as a matter of fact, there was one other thing:

His desire to take back Alice from her imprisonment by the Axiom Church. Even as he stood here swinging his wooden sword, the image of that little blond girl would not disappear from his mind. It had been that way ever since he was chopping at the Gigas Cedar.

That summer day was eight years in the past now.

When the Integrity Knight named Deusolbert Synthesis Seven took Alice away, Eugeo could do nothing but stand and watch. He was holding the Dragonbone Ax capable of cutting through steel, and yet he couldn't even lift it. Even though right nearby, someone…a boy around his age…was screaming, begging Eugeo to act, pleading.

And...who had that boy been, anyway? Eugeo's only friend close enough to scream his name with that kind of passion was Alice. And yet he could practically hear the voice echoing in his ears today.

All these thoughts passed through his mind while an automatic counter kept track of the number of swings he'd done—until a glee-filled voice broke his concentration.

"Well, well, I must say that Eugeo's training always surprises me with its strangeness."

The tip of his sword slipped and landed awkwardly, delivering a nasty shock to his wrists the way it did when he failed to land a clean blow on the Gigas Cedar with his ax.

Eugeo was in the corner of the spacious training hall, while Raios and Humbert were in the middle, so it was no accident that he had overheard the comment so clearly. He'd heard every kind of snarky insult under the sun from them, and it ashamed him to admit that they were still effective. He resumed his exercise, chiding himself to ignore them.

"Eugeo does that each and every night, but I wonder what meaning there can be in simple, dull swinging, without any techniques or forms, Humbert."

"I profess that I wonder the same thing, Raios." They mocked within earshot, chuckling to themselves.

Eugeo did not react physically, but inside his head he retorted, *You seem suspiciously bolder when Kirito isn't around, Raios.*

For some reason, for the last two months, Raios's and Humbert's provocations were totally absent when Kirito was with Eugeo. Instead, they doubled their spite when Eugeo was alone, but the circumstances indicated that it was more out of distaste for Kirito than weakness in Eugeo.

Something must have happened between Kirito and the nobles at the end of their primary year, but Kirito never elaborated on it more than that it was "a little tiff," and Eugeo certainly wasn't going to ask Raios. The only detail that seemed relevant was how after the graduation ceremony, when Kirito presented Sortiliena with a pot of rare blue flowers, Raios and Humbert had been visibly pale when they saw it. Eugeo didn't know what that meant, though.

At any rate, he wasn't going to complain about the fact that Kirito's presence made the noble sons behave. On the other hand, he was an elite disciple now and couldn't hide in the shadow of his partner forever.

In the middle of June next month would be the first testing matches of the school year. The final ranking would be just before graduation, but if Raios and Humbert showed total superiority in the first head-to-head, it didn't bode well for his future chances. The way that Sortiliena had finally overcome the superior Volo Levantein at the last possible chance simply did not *happen*, Golgorosso explained, strangely pleased for an outcome that didn't affect him.

Like Volo, the current first and second seats—Raios and Humbert—had lifelong training in the High-Norkia style of swordsmanship. Their personalities were devoid of any inspirational qualities, but their skill with the blade was head and shoulders above the other nobles. With less than a month to go to the first match, Eugeo had to admit he didn't know what he could do to overcome the challenge they posed.

But at the very least, I can tell myself that you haven't swung your weapon more than I have, he insisted silently, finishing off the four hundred strikes.

He stood up straight, grabbed a towel from his waist, and wiped down the wooden blade, followed by the sweat glistening on his forehead and neck. Eugeo looked back and saw that the two men were still standing in the center of the hall, instructing each other on their forms.

As he faced forward again and exhaled, the Bells of Time-Tolling hanging from the tower of the main school building played the melody for six o'clock—the exact same melody that had played at the church back home. As opposed to the highly regimented primary trainee dorm, the elite disciples were given plenty of leeway to determine their own schedules, and Eugeo was allowed to eat dinner at any time between six and eight o'clock. He could've kept practicing if he wanted, but Kirito was busy studying, and Eugeo had to bring him some food.

Speaking of which, Kirito never specified the dish he wanted. If they're serving those pickled knobblemelons he hates so much, I'll get him extra.

He put the hand towel and wooden sword back in their spots along his waist, then headed for the exit when he heard Raios and Humbert talking as they hung up their swords.

"My word, Disciple Eugeo merely struck the log and didn't bother to practice his forms."

Humbert picked up where he'd left off. "From what I hear, Eugeo was a woodcutter at some miserable rural village. Perhaps the only techniques he knows are meant for logs."

"Well said! As fellow students under the same roof, I suppose it behooves us to at least teach him a proper form."

"Why, Raios, your dedication and generosity are the very image of a nobleman!"

The well-rehearsed farce nearly made Eugeo groan aloud, but he held it in and kept walking.

Then Humbert spoke to him directly. "What do you say, Eugeo? Why don't you take Raios up on his magnanimous offer? You'll never get such a deal again."

Now there was no way to ignore them. If they addressed him directly and he intentionally ignored it, that would be considered impolite. Elite disciples had the right to perform disciplinary punishment on other students, but only to regular primary and secondary trainees. However, this was an unspoken rule and not an explicit one, so it was possible that they might force Eugeo to undergo punishment, too.

He was going to murmur, "No need to go to such lengths for me" and continue on his way, but then a different thought occurred to him: What if this was actually a golden opportunity?

Raios and Humbert were first- and second-seat disciples—the

best and second-best swordsmen at the academy. Kirito constantly reminded Eugeo not to underestimate them, and he did not believe he was.

But there was something about the nobles' strength being rooted in their self-importance that Eugeo could not accept. Their pride in their noble birth, their derision toward students born from common stock or lesser noble houses, their mockery: Was it right that these things could be giving them strength? If he accepted it as truth, wouldn't he be defiling the lessons of respect and love that Sister Azalia, Elder Gasfut, and his old friend Alice had taught him?

Despite the looks of disdain he was getting, Eugeo summoned the minimum of respect—if not love—for Raios and Humbert that he could. But if that attitude was serving only to amplify their pride and self-esteem, and thus strengthen them, what was the point of it? It would be empty.

On the other hand, he was determined not to follow their example and choose a life of insults and mockery...but he had to know before the testing match next month. What was the true nature of this strength born of self-image? Now that they were offering a "lesson," this might be his best chance to find out.

Eugeo had to admit to himself that this was exactly the sort of thing Kirito would come up with. He opened his mouth and said, "You're right...I won't get another chance for this. I gratefully accept your offer and tutelage."

Raios's and Humbert's eyebrows shot up. They hadn't expected that response, but their lips soon curled into sneers. Humbert spread his hands wide and shrieked, "Ha-ha, of course, of course! Then go ahead and demonstrate your form to us. Let's start with an easy one, such as the Third Form of Flames..."

"No, Second Seat Zizek," Eugeo said, raising his hand and choosing his words carefully. "I would hate to waste your valuable tutoring opportunity on a simple form appraisal. I would prefer to receive your blade instruction directly."

"...What?"

The smile faded from Humbert's face. It was replaced by doubt, suspicion as to Eugeo's motive, and the cruelty of a predator toying with its prey.

"Direct…instruction, you say? Should I take that to mean you wish for me to hit you directly, Disciple Eugeo?"

"I would prefer the stop-short method, of course, but I am the one asking for a lesson. It is not my place to dictate the terms."

"Aha, I see, I see. So a first-strike duel would be agreeable, then."

Humbert's slicked-back gray hair seemed to stand on end just a little bit. His already narrow eyes were down to slits now, and their gaze was vicious. Sadistic enjoyment had won out over suspicion at Eugeo's suddenly agreeable manner.

"As the second seat of the academy and a fourth-rank noble, you might say it is my duty to respond when my tutelage is sought. Very well, Disciple Eugeo—I shall demonstrate my style to you."

He promptly yanked his wooden sword from his waist with unnecessary flair. It was made of the same platinum oak as Eugeo's, but his had fine patterns carved into the sides. Next to Humbert, Raios started to say something, but he reconsidered and clamped his mouth shut. He smiled easily, retreated three mels, and nodded to Humbert when he turned back to look.

Emboldened by the approval of his partner, Humbert pointed his blade straight at Eugeo, who was standing still with his arms at his sides, and shouted, "Here I come! Feel the full might of the High-Norkia style!"

He spread his legs front and rear and pulled the sword back with his right hand until it rested upon his shoulder. This was the stance for Lightning Slash, the ultimate attack of the Norkia sword style. Oddly, it wasn't Mountain-Splitting Wave, which was the corresponding attack for the actual *High*-Norkia style he mentioned. Surely he hadn't held back out of concern for Eugeo—he was probably just hesitant to show off his best moves.

Still, Lightning Slash was not an attack to be overlooked. Even a dull wooden sword could knock you unconscious and wipe out half your life if it struck your skull. It was a terrible taboo to decrease the life of others, of course, but in a consensual duel, the first blow was essentially free. And Humbert obviously had no intention of holding back.

The second seat's decorated practice sword glowed blue, an impressively short period between pose and activation. But Eugeo could completely predict the trajectory the blade would follow; Lightning Slash was identical to Vertical, one of the many secret skills of the Aincrad style.

"*Sheyaah!!*" Humbert screeched. His sword bolted.

But Eugeo was already on the move. He drew his sword from the left, paused, and activated an attack of his own—he would receive the overhead smash with an upward diagonal slice, the Aincrad style's Slant.

Strangely, all the attacks Kirito had taught him were not in the common language but the strange and foreign sacred tongue. Even Kirito didn't know why. It probably had something to do with his missing memories from before he appeared in Rulid as a "lost child of Vecta," so it was a very lucky thing that he hadn't forgotten the skills themselves.

Like Lightning Slash, Slant was a one-part skill, but its versatility lay in how it was effectively bidirectional: you could swing it from upper right to lower left or from lower left to upper right. In the latter case, the stance allowed him to draw and activate directly from his left hip, which drastically shortened the time required.

Normally, if one waited for the opponent to start a skill attack before reacting, the only choice would be to leap out of the way—and even that rarely worked. But Eugeo timed his Slant to start just after Humbert's, the sword leaving a blue trail in the air as it swept upward to smash against the Lightning Slash. The resulting light and sound were nothing like one would expect from pieces of wood.

"Whoa..." Humbert grunted. The surprise on his face gave way to anger, and he pressed down hard. The dark- and light-blue glows infusing the swords were still active. As soon as one of them got pushed back a few cens, the attack would conclude and give way to the other. Eugeo tensed his legs, willing his sword to stay put and swing through.

The wood creaked and cracked, and Humbert's sword gave way slightly. The dark-blue glow of Lightning Slash flickered, suggesting its imminent demise.

I knew it—in a simple competition of strength, I'm superior!

He'd expected this, but seeing the proof in action strengthened Eugeo's resolve. He couldn't match the nobles' precise image control, which extended down to the very angle of their fingers and toes, but he knew that swinging that heavy ax two thousand times a day in the forest gave him physical strength. Even Golgorosso, with his steel-like muscles, said that Eugeo was "slight but well trained."

Some of the nobles trained in the High-Norkia style liked to label common-born Golgorosso's Baltio style as rural swordsmanship from the sticks, but in a proper duel—not the practiced beauty of form demonstrations—arm strength was a formidable weapon on its own. And Kirito's free-flowing Aincrad style gave Eugeo the flexibility to lock blades in any circumstance.

Even if I don't yet have that "something" I can imbue my sword with, the technique and strength I've built up are enough to match any noble's! Eugeo told himself, summoning all the muscle he could.

But at just that moment, Humbert's expression swiftly morphed into one of rage. "Don't get...cocky!"

His eyes and brows shot up as far as they would go, and a metallic screech escaped between his clenched, bared teeth. Suddenly, the nearly faded blue light pulsed back, dark and ugly.

This time, it was Eugeo's blade that creaked. The weight on his right arm doubled, and fierce pain shot through his wrist and shoulder. The two cens of advantage he'd held slipped away until their positioning in the clash was where it started.

Where is this strength coming from?! Eugeo wondered, just barely holding his ground. Humbert couldn't have this kind of physical strength, not with the way he always preened and practiced his forms without ever breaking a real sweat. So if it wasn't physical might…it had to be the "strength of self-image" that Kirito talked about. Apparently, his point of view that he was naturally superior to others was powerful enough to overcome all of Eugeo's steady discipline.

He couldn't believe it. He just couldn't bring himself to believe that Stacia, goddess of creation, would implement this law of the universe.

Just then, Humbert's hair bristled, and he hissed, "Did you really think you could break me with that cheap sneak attack?"

"Ch-cheap…?"

"Of course it is. You pretended you would let yourself get hit, then pulled out that technique without any form or stance at all. If that's not cheap, what is?"

"N-no! That's just part and parcel of my style…the Aincrad style!" Eugeo shot back without thinking. If the High-Norkia style placed emphasis on the power and visual of the technique, then the Aincrad style was a practical one that prioritized landing the blow above all else. Of course its skills launched quicker, as it had combination attacks that the other sword schools did not.

The concept of the Aincrad style was exemplified by the life of Kirito, its only adherent. Never bragging, never for show, simply moving headlong toward the goal. Hit a wall and bounce back, again and again. If it weren't for him, Eugeo would never have even reached Zakkaria, much less Centoria.

So Eugeo's reaction to Humbert's assessment of the style was instantaneous. However, the mental response rebounded into his physical body, such that his sword weakened a bit. This time, it was the pale-blue glow surrounding Eugeo's blade that flickered. He spread his legs, bent back his upper half, and desperately stood his ground.

Humbert leered. In a voice like fingers scraping glass, he jeered,

"The miserable cheapness of your style is apparent from your predicament. Perhaps you thought you'd take over Raios's position or mine in the next testing matches…Well, think again. I'm going to shatter your shoulder so that you won't swing a sword for a good long while."

"*Rrgh…!*"

He gritted his teeth, but Humbert's sword only got heavier. Even when it met resistance, a sword technique could hold its power for quite a while as long as it was still located in the original path, but the direct vertical pressure of Humbert's Lightning Slash was pushing him away from the proper trajectory. One more cen—five milices, even—would spell the end of his Slant and doom him to that shoulder wound.

The Swordcraft Academy had an excellent medical facility, of course, replete with healing herbs and an attendant healer with expert knowledge of sacred arts. But there was a limit to what they could do, and unless they used a dangerous art like pouring one's life directly into that of the injured, there was no way to instantly heal a broken bone, for example. If he suffered such a wound now, he wouldn't be able to participate in next month's testing match…

How stupid am I? What swordsman fears injury?!

Eugeo dismissed the fear creeping into his heart and focused his mind on his sword.

He could have chosen to ignore the taunts. It had been his idea to make it a duel. Now he was in danger of losing, rattled by the opponent's words—how pathetic could he get? He had drawn his blade; after that, he could only use his skill and strength to his best efforts and accept the consequences. That was the mentality of the Aincrad style.

And I still haven't given him everything I've got.

He focused not on Humbert's sadistic grin but on the wooden sword gripped in his right hand. The firmness and weight of the oak, its curve and grain registered in his arm—he could even feel the faint vibration of the Slant's dying power.

Make yourself one with the sword, his friend and teacher, Kirito, would always say.

Eugeo couldn't manage that yet, but thanks to his everyday practice, he could on very rare occasions hear what seemed like the voice of the sword. A voice that said, *Not that way, move like this instead.*

This was one of those moments.

If he continued to receive the overhand swing from below, he would inevitably be overpowered. A change in technique was needed.

"...Rah!" Eugeo bellowed, a rarity for him. He flicked his wrist, catching Humbert's sword on the right flat of his own. That action ended his Slant, giving the Lightning Slash a free path toward his right shoulder, roaring bluish-black as it descended.

In one smooth motion, Eugeo slid his sword back atop his shoulder. Immediately, that triggered the Aincrad style's Vertical.

Humbert's blade caught the right sleeve of the practice jacket, tearing several cens of the dark-blue fabric.

Suddenly, Eugeo's sword flashed a brilliant blue again and rocketed back against Humbert with tremendous force.

"Nwah!"

His eyes went wide at this unexpected response. Humbert and Raios knew about the Aincrad style's combination attacks by now, but they wouldn't have predicted that they could chain one ultimate attack with another. Even Eugeo hadn't known about the possibility; he simply moved as his body willed.

Humbert's sword shot back over fifty cens, the light of the Lightning Slash fading promptly. He lost his balance, and his feet came off the floor.

But fortunately for him—and perhaps for Eugeo—by not staying firm and suffering a blow to the left shoulder, Humbert himself was launched through the air and flew over three mels backward.

A fall would certainly end the duel in Eugeo's favor, but to Humbert's stubborn credit, he managed to land on his feet and avoid toppling. He leaned as far as he possibly could, just to keep his balance.

Eugeo knew that if he followed up, he could easily land a blow, but before he could regain his footing, a crisp voice filled the training hall.

"That is enough. We will consider this a draw," said Raios Antinous theatrically, a smile playing on his red lips.

Humbert stood up straight again and shouted, "B-but, Raios! I...I would never draw with this bumpkin of a—!"

"Humbert," the first seat reprimanded softly. The other youth abruptly bowed his head. He transferred his sword to his left side and raised his right fist to his chest—the knight's salute—then turned on his heel without waiting for Eugeo's response.

From Humbert's left, Raios glanced at him with that wan smile and made a show of applauding. "Your bizarre techniques were quite entertaining, Disciple Eugeo. Perhaps you should consider petitioning the Imperial Circus for a new calling after graduation."

"...Your advice is appreciated, Disciple Antinous," Eugeo replied, intentionally omitting the "first seat" title, but Raios merely nodded amiably and turned for the exit. Humbert followed him, glaring at Eugeo for all he was worth.

Raios's soft leather practice shoes squeaked on the polished floor as he walked. But just as he passed Eugeo in the center of the hall, he paused and murmured, "Next time, I'll show you the might of a noble house."

"...Nothing stopping you from doing it now," Eugeo retorted, but in truth, he was exhausted after his four hundred swings and the impromptu duel.

Raios merely smirked and continued walking, only to utter an even quieter, "Waving your sword around is not all there is to battle, you nameless buffoon."

The first seat continued on his way with a chuckle, followed by the furious Humbert, who passed without comment. Eventually, Eugeo heard the door open and close behind him.

Amid the fresh silence, Eugeo breathed long and deep.

A strength based on a noble's regard for himself. In his first experience face-to-face with it, Eugeo found that it was much heavier than he expected. If he'd stuck to his Slant, he would have failed and ended up with a broken bone in his shoulder. Part of it was the disadvantage of blocking an overhead strike from below, but that wasn't all of it. Humbert's disdain and mockery of Eugeo's class was like a curse that bound his blade and limbs.

The Aincrad style's flexibility in producing ultimate techniques from various stances got him out of trouble this time, but tricks and sneakiness weren't going to help him through all of the upcoming test matches throughout the year. There would come times when he needed to win head-on through sheer strength.

Eugeo had to find something by then. Something he could put into his blade that could counteract the boundless self-confidence that Humbert and Raios wielded.

He lifted the practice sword and traced the wood that he'd treated to such abuse.

"...Thanks. Hope you'll help me out next time, too."

Then he put it back on his waist and started walking, just as the bells chimed a quick count for six thirty. Kirito was bound to be getting hungry during his cram session back at the room. Eugeo crossed the pale floorboards, gave the empty training hall a brief salute, then headed for the cafeteria.

After a short hallway, he was back in the elite disciple dorm. There were no private rooms on the first floor, which was reserved for the bathing hall, the cafeteria, and meeting rooms.

In the primary trainee dorm, meals were at fixed times with preplanned daily menus, but the disciples had much more freedom in both regards. The mess hall was open from six to eight, and the cook there would prepare any of a number of rotating dishes to the students' needs. Not only that, you could eat it there or take it back to your room if you wanted.

Fortunately, Raios and Humbert must have gone into the bath, as the cafeteria was empty. Eugeo walked up to the kitchen counter and checked the day's menu. The choices for main dish were roast mutton, fried fish, and boiled chicken dumplings.

Let's see…He'd want the dumplings, a big serving of cheesy vegetables, the pickled ori nuts, and some ice-cold siral water.

Disgruntled that he somehow knew his partner well enough to identify his ideal meal out of the possible choices, Eugeo leaned over the counter to shout into the back.

"Good evening! I'd like two servings to go. For the first one, I'll have…"

2

Eugeo was prepared for any kind of petty revenge scheme, but for the next few days after the impromptu duel, Raios and Humbert stayed quiet.

When he passed them at the disciples' dorm or the central building, Humbert would give him a hateful look, but not so much as a word otherwise. Just in case, he told Kirito about the incident at the training hall and warned him to be on guard, but the nobles hadn't bothered him at all.

"It seems so strange...They're not the kind of guys who would withdraw and mind their own business after that. And what Raios said sure sounded like a promise for retribution," Eugeo muttered, leaning back into a leather couch.

Across from him, Kirito held a ceramic cup to his lips. "I don't think they've had a sudden change of heart, either. But if you think about it, it's got to be difficult to pull off their kind of trick here at this dorm."

He sipped his cofil tea, black and unsweetened. It was nine thirty at night after a wild week, with the day of rest ahead. They'd finished with their daily practice, dinner, and bath, and at this time on a weekday, they'd be in their beds sleeping—but it had become their custom to spend this one night a week in the common room, sipping tea and talking things over.

Eugeo lifted his own cup, tasted the hot black liquid, and made a face. His partner loved this powdered tea from the southern empire and always prepared it when it was his turn to make the tea, but Eugeo found it too bitter to drink straight. He poured in a large amount of milk from the jar and stirred it in with the little spoon, glancing at Kirito.

The gesture apparently prompted Kirito to ask an unexpected question. "When you were a kid back home in Rulid, what kind of pranks would you play around the school?"

Eugeo took another sip of the cofil tea, which was no longer bitter but rich and fragrant. He shrugged. "I was usually the one on the receiving end. You remember Zink, the chief man-at-arms, who challenged me to a fight before we left? He used to harass me all the time…Hiding my shoes, putting itch-bugs in my lunch, teasing me for hanging out with Alice."

"Ha-ha-ha, I guess kids do the same things in every world… But he didn't hit you or anything like that. Right?"

"Of course not," Eugeo said, wide-eyed. "He could never do such a thing. I mean—"

"The Taboo Index forbids it, exactly. 'Thou shalt not intentionally damage the life of another without a reason listed elsewhere.' But…is it okay to hide someone's shoes? Isn't stealing also a terrible taboo?"

"Stealing means to take another's possessions and make them your own without permission. It takes twenty-four hours for the sacred text in the Stacia Window that indicates ownership to pass from person to person once the item has been moved or placed in the other's home. That's why, even if you have an agreement to give something to another person, you can still fairly request its return within the day. And if it's removed without permission, you can place the item anywhere that's not your own home, which will not overwrite the ownership and thus doesn't count as stealing. You aren't telling me…you've forgotten such a basic tenet of the law, are you?"

Eugeo stared at Kirito, the infamous lost child of Vecta,

but the other boy merely ruffled his black hair and laughed in embarrassment.

"Oh, r-right, of course. No, I haven't forgotten. I remember... but wait. What about in that story, then? When Bercouli tried to steal the Blue Rose Sword from the dragon's lair—wasn't that breaking a taboo?"

"A dragon isn't a person."

"Ah...gotcha."

"Back on topic, while it's not a taboo to hide someone's belongings for a prank, if left out in the open on nobody's territory, the item's life will start to dwindle, so if it's not returned before then, that's damage to another's property. So no matter what, my shoes would always be back by the evening. But...what does this have to do with Raios and Humbert behaving themselves?" Eugeo wondered.

Kirito blinked, apparently forgetting that he had brought it up in the first place, then said, "Ah, r-right. Um, so my point is, this school has a bunch of its own rules in addition to the Taboo Index, right? And there's an entry about going into the private rooms of other students or faculty without permission. That means they can't get in here, and all our property is inside our room. We'd have to forget something important out in a public... space..."

He trailed off for some reason, but then regained his train of thought. "And we haven't done that, of course. So it's essentially impossible for Raios and Humbert to play pranks on us the same way that Zink picked on poor little Eugeo back in Rulid Village."

"Don't you 'poor little' me. Hmm...but now that you mention it, I guess you're right that at the disciples' dorm, there's no way to harass someone worse than simple insults."

"And if the insult crosses a line, it becomes subject to disciplinary punishment," Kirito added, grinning.

Disciplinary punishment was a special right of the elite disciples, a kind of staff-proxy authority to uphold the rules. If a student committed some rudeness or slight that was not against the rules but deemed worthy of discipline, the elite disciple could choose to punish the student at his or her own discretion. Kirito himself had recently been the subject of this system, when he got mud on the uniform of Volo Levantein, previous first seat of the academy. Volo used his disciplinary punishment privilege to challenge Kirito to a duel.

This privilege was customarily used on primary and secondary trainees, but there was no stipulation in the school rules that it couldn't be used against another disciple. So it was theoretically possible for a disciple to punish another disciple, and this was the reason that Raios's and Humbert's japes and insults had decreased since the new school year started.

Kirito's cup was empty, so Eugeo poured him some more tea. This time, his partner drizzled a little milk into it. He swirled the delicate silver spoon with his fingertips, lost in thought.

Eventually, Kirito said, "If they can't mess with our stuff, then they'll have to go after us. The most direct method would be starting a duel and landing a blow, but you've already proven you can work a draw against them. The only other thing I can imagine is...tempting me with promises of wealth and turning me against you."

"Huh...?" Eugeo whimpered, then clamped his mouth shut.

But Kirito smirked and boasted, "Have no fear, young man. Big Bro will never abandon you."

"I—I wasn't worried about that! But if not money...I wonder if a big plate of Gottoro's special meat buns would tempt you."

"That would definitely work," Kirito admitted, deadly serious, then laughed. "But enough jokes. I think we can rule out the likelihood that they'll try to mess with us or our belongings."

Then his expression got tense again. "But that does mean they could try anything that doesn't fall under the Taboo Index or school rules. I highly doubt they have any intention of handing over the first and second seat...Let me know if there's anything we're overlooking, Eugeo."

"Yeah, I'll think about it. It's less than a month to the first

testing match, after all. We need to make sure we're in the best possible condition to face them."

"Right…On the other hand, maybe they were threatening us with no intent to follow up, just to keep us nervous and on edge. Don't lose your head—stay cool!" Kirito proclaimed, draining his cup.

Eugeo looked confused. "What do you mean? Stay…cool?"

For some reason, Kirito averted his eyes guiltily and cleared his throat. "Err, that's…a mantra of the Aincrad style. I guess you could say it means 'be calm.' You can also use it as a farewell."

"Ahh, I see. I'll have to remember that. Stay cool, stay cool," Eugeo repeated. The unfamiliar phrase was in the same sacred tongue as the special Aincrad techniques, but he found it surprisingly comfortable once he tried it out. He repeated it over and over under his breath, until Kirito started looking awkward and clapped his hands together.

"Well! The ten o'clock bells will ring soon, so I guess we should call it a night. As for tomorrow, I actually have an errand to run…"

"Oh no you don't, Kirito. You can't slip your way out of this one," Eugeo said, setting down his cup and glaring at his partner.

On tomorrow's day of rest, they were supposed to take their pages, Tiese and Ronie, on a little friendship-building field trip—which would still be within the school grounds. Based on Kirito's reaction when the idea was brought up, Eugeo had been expecting him to come up with some reason to weasel his way out of it.

"Listen, it's been a month now since we started tutoring those two. Sortiliena was nice to you last year when you were her page, right?"

"Whenever we weren't training, yes. Wow…that name brings back memories. I wonder how she's doing…"

"Don't go off into a flashback. My point is, now it's your turn to be the good tutor. They're coming over at nine in the morning, so make sure you're ready by then!" Eugeo commanded, jabbing a finger at Kirito. He gave an easy affirmative and got up from the couch.

They took their dishes over to the sink in the corner of the room, with Kirito rinsing off each piece while Eugeo handled the drying. In Rulid and Zakkaria, they had to draw the water from a well, but in Centoria, nearly all buildings had metal pipes that brought crisp, clean water with just the twist of a faucet. Eugeo thought at first it was the work of a Divine Object like the Bells of Time-Tolling, but it turned out that each district of the series had a huge reservoir well infused with wind-element sacred arts that applied pressure to push it through all the many pipes.

So the water they got was always fresh, and they didn't have to worry about it degrading in its bucket. If they'd had this back in Rulid, how delighted would the children be that they didn't have to go out and draw water each morning? Eugeo considered this as he finished up washing and put the cups back in the cupboard.

Kirito drank a few deep gulps straight from the tap at the end, wiped his lips, and yawned. "Okay, wake me up at eight o'clock, then. Good night, Eugeo."

"Eight is too late! Seven thirty! Good night, Kirito," he replied, then remembered something and added, "Stay cool."

His partner turned to look over his shoulder with a smirk, just short of his bedroom door, and said, "Listen, I know I said that it's a farewell of sorts, but not before bed every night. Save it for a proper parting."

"Sheesh, this saying is more complicated than I thought. Fine…see you tomorrow, then."

"Later," Kirito said, waving and retreating into his room. Eugeo blew out the lamp on the wall and opened the door on the opposite wall.

His bedroom was nearly half the size of the ten-man rooms at the primary dorm. There wasn't a spot of dust on the floor after Tiese's cleaning earlier. He changed into his white pajamas and flopped down onto his soft bed.

As sleep snuck up on his mind, a portion of the earlier conversation came with it, for some mysterious reason.

But that does mean they could try anything that doesn't fall under the Taboo Index or school rules.

It was what Kirito said about Raios and Humbert. Eugeo had agreed with him at the time, but it was a way of thinking he found very hard to accept.

From his childhood until now, between the Rulid Village standards, the Zakkaria Garrison bylaws, and now the Swordcraft Academy rules, Eugeo had peered here and there for shortcuts. But he had never once attempted to find a way around the Taboo Index, the greatest set of laws in all of humanity—except that, yes, he *had*.

It happened eight years ago, when the Integrity Knight landed at the village to take Alice away. Eugeo set upon the knight with the Dragonbone Ax in an attempt to save her—except that he couldn't move a step. Even now, recalling the incident caused the inside of his right eye to twitch.

He didn't contain an ounce of rebellion against the Integrity Knights or the Church now, of course. The knight had taken Alice away as dictated by the law, so Eugeo would follow that same law to pass through the gate of the church and meet her again. That was why he had left home and come this far.

But if Kirito was right, and Raios and Humbert would try "anything that doesn't fall under the Taboo Index," did that mean that the absolute book of laws, the system put in place at the very creation of the world, was merely something they reluctantly obeyed? In their heart of hearts, was the Taboo Index something they found annoying, distasteful?

Surely even *they* wouldn't go that far. The Taboo Index could not even be doubted. It was the ultimate tome of justice and fairness, equally applied to a common man and to an emperor.

Eugeo bit his lip as he lifted his gaze to the ceiling, lit with the pale reflection of the moonlight. If one were allowed to defy the Index, then what did that say about his own failure to stop the

Integrity Knight from taking Alice, and then spending the next six years chopping away at the Gigas Cedar? What had he been upholding, and to what purpose?

The core of his right eye twinged again. He squeezed his lids shut, driving away the conflicted thoughts, and allowed himself to slide into an uneasy sleep.

The Swordcraft Academy grounds, surrounded by tall steel fences, contained a forest that occupied a third of its space. The ancient trees were covered in golden moss, and the way the sun filtered down to the green undergrowth reminded Eugeo of home, but being located so much farther south meant that the wildlife was more varied. Here and there were new creatures he'd never seen up north soaking up the sun: tiny foxes, for instance, or long, narrow snakes colored blue-green. He'd been here over a year now, but the sight still fascinated him.

"Are you listening, Eugeo?" said a voice at his side. He turned with a start.

"Sorry, sorry, of course I am. You were saying?"

"So you *weren't* listening!" said the girl with long hair the color of ripe red apples—Eugeo's trainee page, Tiese Schtrinen.

He turned away from her eyes, which were the same brilliant color as her hair, and awkwardly said, "The...the forest was so beautiful, I got distracted...I haven't seen some of these animals before."

"Is that so?" Tiese asked, following his line of sight and then shrugging when she saw what he was looking at. "Oh, that's just a golden flying fox. You can find them in just about any tree growing around the city."

"Oh...That's right—you grew up here, didn't you? Is your house close by?"

"My family lives in District Eight, so it's a bit of a hike from District Five."

"Ah, I see...Hmm?"

Eugeo paused and turned to Tiese. The primary trainee uniform, which he'd thought a bit ugly when he wore it last year, seemed strangely fresh and refined on her. That made sense; if they hadn't been fellow students, frontier child Eugeo would never have any connection to someone like her.

"Tiese, you're a noble, right? I thought I heard that all the noble mansions were concentrated in Districts Three and Four," Eugeo said politely.

Tiese ducked her head in embarrassment, then shook it, "Technically, my father's a sixth-rank peer...but we're barely lower nobles as it is. Only the fourth-rank and higher nobles can live in the areas near the imperial government. There are lots of restrictions on the fifth- and sixth-rank nobles. Father likes to say, 'I wish we were commoners; at least they don't have to fear the higher nobles' judicial authority'...Oh! Oh my goodness, I'm so sorry..."

She bowed, ashamed that she'd said something she considered rude to Eugeo, whose entire family tree was common.

"Don't worry about it. Besides, I thought all nobles had that judicial authority thing," he said, recalling the Basic Imperial Law he'd had to study last year.

"Not at all!" Tiese protested. "Judicial authority only extends down to fourth-rank. The lower nobles are actually subject to the judicial review of the higher ones. My father's a scribe for the government, and he says that many of the fifth- and sixth-rank nobles working at the palace and government building have been punished for upsetting higher nobles over some insignificant thing or another. Of course, they're civilized adults, so it's not physical punishment but docked pay and things like that."

"Oh, I see...I didn't realize things could be that hard for nobility, too," Eugeo murmured, surprised.

The red-haired trainee blushed for some reason and added rapidly, "M-my point is, being the heir to a sixth-rank noble house is noble in name alone. Our lifestyle is pretty much the same as any regular family."

"Ohhh..."

Eugeo couldn't affirm or deny this, only murmur vaguely. He considered the workings of the empire.

The government's Basic Imperial Law laid out the structure of Norlangarthian society. But because the higher Taboo Index covered all crimes and punishments, the imperial law mostly dealt with the regulations of the various classes of citizens—in other words, the rights of the nobles and the rights of the common people.

In the law class of their first year (the only other academic subjects were sacred arts and history), a certain black-haired student had asked the elderly teacher why the empire had nobles and commoners.

As a lower noble himself, the teacher was initially at a loss for words. Then he said firmly, "According to the prophecies passed down by the Axiom Church since time immemorial, one day the forces of darkness will invade through the four great passages: the Northern Cave, the Western Ravine, the Southern Corridor, and the Eastern Gate. In order to vanquish the subhuman scourge, all those in the four empires who have the calling of guards and soldiers must rise up to fight as the army of humanity. Our nobility hone their skill, learn sacred arts, and discipline their minds and bodies so that they may lead those forces."

While Eugeo was thrilled and moved by this answer, part of him was still conflicted. Two years ago, Eugeo and Kirito had fought a band of goblins in that very Northern Cave the teacher mentioned. Sadly, the goblin captain had knocked him out in the midst of the fight, but the terrifying appearances and raspy, bestial voices of the creatures were still vivid in his memory. He and Kirito decided never to mention the incident while at school. If they did, he suspected that half the female students might pass out in fright.

Eugeo never wanted to repeat that experience, of course. So he was extremely impressed by the bravery of the nobles to stand at the lead and battle those goblins and the even more fearsome orcs and ogres.

On the other hand, 380 years had passed since Stacia created the world. In all that time, the forces of darkness had never once invaded the human realm. The higher nobles of the four empires were freed from their daily labor, lived in huge mansions, and even used their judicial authority on lower nobles—all for this supposed preparation against an enemy they'd never seen and whose arrival was uncertain...

Tiese seemed to read Eugeo's mind. She sighed and said, "As I'm the eldest child, Father is hoping that by putting me into this school, I might be conferred a fourth-rank title by the time I take over the house, so that I won't be subject to judicial authority. If I'm chosen as the academy's representative and get far in the Imperial Battle Tournament, it might not be out of the question... But given that I was only eleventh on the entrance exam rankings, I suppose it might be pointless to hope."

She stuck out her tongue and grinned. Eugeo had to narrow his eyes, she felt so radiant to him. He'd come here on a very personal quest—to reunite with his childhood friend—but Tiese was learning swordfighting for the purpose of improving her family's lot in life. In a way, she seemed to embody the true glory of nobility.

"No, Tiese...You're doing great. You worked so hard to make your father happy that you achieved a place in the top twelve primary trainees," Eugeo told her, full of emotion.

"Oh, n-no!" she shrieked. "I just got lucky that the demonstration portion happened to line up with my own expertise. And my rank came after a lifetime of training, ever since I was three years old. What you're doing is *way* more impressive. It's hard enough to get here on a garrison recommendation, and not only did you succeed at that, you're now the fifth seat disciple. I'm actually really honored to be your page."

"Aw, geez..."

He bobbed his head and lifted a hand to ruffle his bangs in embarrassment, then realized it was exactly the sort of thing Kirito would do and quickly took his hand down.

Tiese claimed that it was an "honor" to be his page, but for her and Eugeo, and Ronie and Kirito, the matchups were more like the guidance of Stacia: in other words, total coincidence.

The elite disciples determined the pages' assignments by taking their pick, in order of rank. That meant that as first seat, Raios picked his page out of the top twelve new students first, then Humbert. Eugeo would be fifth and Kirito sixth. But oddly enough, the two talked it over and decided to wait until the end. They wanted the two students whom none of the other ten disciples picked.

In other words, the two options left to them at the end were Tiese and Ronie. They both seemed at a loss for words when they realized it was two girls—Kirito looked especially uneasy—but Eugeo was ultimately glad for it. After all, the sole, pitiful reason none of the other disciples had chosen the girls was because they were the only sixth-rank nobles of the bunch.

The girls had no idea what went on during the choosing process, and the boys had no reason to tell them. Eugeo was happy with Tiese as his page, and Kirito was...probably the same way with Ronie.

So Eugeo cleared his throat and switched topics to his own experience. "Actually, I didn't have an easy time getting into the academy. I was super nervous. In fact, it was half because of Kirito that I made it in and got to be an elite disciple this year..."

Tiese blinked, her eyes the color of leaves reddening in the autumn. "What?! So Kirito's...better than you?"

"...I'm finding it very difficult to say 'yes' when you phrase it that way..."

Tiese laughed pleasantly, and he looked over his shoulder, worried that his partner wasn't actually at his page's side after all. Fortunately, he soon heard Kirito's voice on the breeze.

"...So you see, when they attack with a high slash in the High-Norkia style, there are basically only two trajectories you need to prepare for—either straight overhead or diagonal from the top right. Anything else and they'll need to change their footing, so you'll have time to adjust accordingly. As for how to choose between overhead or top-right..."

Well, it might be dry, but at least Ronie seems to be listening to him, Eugeo noted with a smirk, and looked forward again.

So his reason for learning the sword was to reunite with Alice, and Tiese's and Ronie's were to improve the standing of their families. Meanwhile, at every opportunity, Kirito claimed that his goal was the same as Eugeo's.

Eugeo wasn't going to doubt his friendship, but there were times that he felt that Kirito's reason for practicing wasn't to gain some tangible goal but purely to master the art of the blade. Such was the perfect mesh of Kirito's personality and his Aincrad style. They were practically one and the same.

So far, Eugeo had focused his attention solely on Raios and Humbert in preparation for the official matches next month. But it occurred to him now that, depending on how the matches played out, he might end up facing off against his good friend and teacher.

He couldn't win, of course. But more importantly, he couldn't even imagine crossing swords with Kirito and giving him a serious fight. How would he summon strength into his blade? How would he execute his techniques against a friend...?

"Oh, how about the side of the pond there?" Tiese said suddenly, pointing ahead and rousing Eugeo from his thoughts. He followed her slender fingers to a thick, short bed of grass along the bank of a beautiful pond. It was the perfect place to set out a picnic.

"Yeah, that looks good. Hey, Kirito, Ronie! Let's have lunch next to the pond here!" Eugeo shouted over his shoulder. His best friend gave him that typical dazzling smile and waved.

The four of them laid out their blanket on the grass and sat down in a little circle.

"Ahh...I'm so hungry," Kirito complained, rubbing his stomach theatrically. The girls giggled and opened their picnic basket to set up the food.

"Um, we made it ourselves, so I hope you like it," said Ronie Arabel, primary trainee, as she shyly set out the plates. She wasn't nearly as nervous as she usually was. Eugeo was hoping that through this leisure activity, she would finally realize that the black-clad elite disciple was hardly as imposing as he looked, and then eventually get used to his tutelage.

Inside the large basket was a veritable feast of white-bread sandwiches packed with thinly sliced meat, fish, cheese, and herbs; fragrant fried chicken; and cake packed with dried fruit and nuts.

Tiese examined the remaining life of each dish, then Ronie led a premeal prayer of "Avi Admina." The words were barely out of their mouths before Kirito was reaching for the food. He stuffed a large hunk of meat into his mouth, closed his eyes, and chewed, then spoke in the tones of a teacher.

"Ah, quite good. In fact, Ronie and Tiese, I might go so far as to say that this is the equal of the Jumping Deer."

"Wow, really?!" the girls exclaimed, their faces shining. They shared a glance and burst into smiles. Eugeo took a thin sandwich of dried fish and herbs and dug in.

Unlike the rustic food that Alice would bring to Eugeo every day in the forest back home, this bread was white and thickly buttered, a treat from the big city. When he first came here, the refined taste was too much for Eugeo's simple palette, but he thoroughly enjoyed it now. He wondered if he was just getting used to something different.

"It's really good, Tiese. Wasn't it hard to get all these ingredients, though?"

"Uh…well, actually…" she mumbled, glancing over at Ronie, who explained.

"As you know, primary trainees are only allowed to leave the academy on days of rest, so we asked Kirito to go buy the ingredients at the central market after class yesterday. You were busy in the library at the time, so…"

"Oh…oh, I see," Eugeo replied, stunned. He glanced over at

Kirito, who was still chowing down. "I would have gone shopping if you'd just told me…And Kirito, if you're that comfortable around them, you don't need to keep running away anymore! What was the point of all this trouble…?" he wondered, both relieved and annoyed. He reached out for the biggest slice of fruitcake and shoved it into his mouth.

"Hey, I was going to eat that," Kirito complained. "Anyway, if anything, I was making things easier on you, Disciple Eugeo."

"Well, you needn't have bothered," Eugeo grumbled. He turned to Tiese and Ronie, who were watching in wide-eyed surprise, and groused, "He's always been like this. Before we joined the garrison in Zakkaria, and on the road here to Centoria, he always starts off as the target of suspicion or fear, and then the next thing you know, the wife and kids at the farm or inn are all hanging out with him and passing him treats. Be careful that he doesn't use this trick on you, too, Ronie."

However, his warning was probably too late. The girl with the burnt-brown hair shook her head, her cheeks darkening. "Oh, no, it's not a trick…Kirito might look scary, but I learned right away that he's really very kind…"

"Oh, and the same for you, Eugeo," Tiese hastily added. He gave her a weak smile and took another bite of cake.

Out of the corner of his eye, he could see his partner chewing smugly, and he started to wonder if there was some way he could get one over on Kirito—when suddenly Tiese and Ronie stretched and sat up formally.

"Um…Eugeo, Kirito, as a matter of fact, we have a request."

"Y-you do? What kind?" Eugeo asked.

Tiese ducked her head humbly, red hair waving. "Well, it's really hard to say this, but…it's about what you mentioned the other day, putting in a good word with the school management about changing tutors…"

"Wh-what?" He gaped, trying to recall the conversation in question. But it quickly came back to him: A few days ago, while Ronie was waiting for Kirito to come back, he might have mentioned something to her about asking a teacher to get her switched to a different disciple, if she wanted.

So this lavish picnic feast was a commemoration for their parting, he realized gloomily. But he needed to be sure. "So, um...does that mean you want to stop being my page...? Or Kirito's...or both of us?"

Ronie and Tiese looked up, momentarily stunned, then shook their heads violently. On Eugeo's left, Tiese leaned over and protested, "N-no! It's not us—not at all! In fact, a bunch of others wish they could switch with *us*...Er, never mind. I mean, it's another girl from our dorm room who wants to switch. Her name's Frenica, and she's very honest, hardworking, and humble despite her skill..."

Tiese's shoulders slumped, and Ronie took over the explanation. "As a matter of fact...the elite disciple who chose Frenica as a page is apparently quite harsh. The last few days, even the most innocent little mistake ends up with hours of discipline, and she's being forced to do things on school grounds that are somewhat inappropriate. It's really weighing on the poor thing..."

The trainees clutched their fists to their chests, red and brown eyes welling with moisture. Eugeo put the half-eaten chicken down on his plate and looked at them, barely able to believe it.

"B-but...even elite disciples shouldn't be able to force their pages to obey commands that are outside the school rules..."

"That's true. They're not being ordered to do things that break the rules, but it's not as though every possible activity is covered...It's a whole bunch of orders that aren't against the rules but are very difficult for a female student to bear..." Tiese said, her voice trailing off into a mumble, cheeks crimson. Eugeo could guess as to what kind of things this disciple was ordering poor Frenica to do.

"It's okay, you don't have to explain any further. I'd love to help you make things better for Frenica. But..."

He consulted the list of school rules inside his head before continuing, "Let's see...'In order to maximize the elite disciple's training, he shall receive a page to address his needs. The page shall be chosen from among the twelve highest-ranking primary trainees of that year, but if the disciple and managing instructor agree, a page can be released and a new one may be chosen.' That means that for Frenica to be reassigned, she needs not only the instructor's consent but that of the disciple in question, too. Still, I can try to plead her case. What's the disciple's name?"

Eugeo felt an ominous foreboding as soon as the words left his mouth. Tiese hesitated, then awkwardly admitted, "It's…Second Seat Humbert Zizek."

The moment she said it, Kirito perked up his ears and groaned. "You mean even after he challenged Eugeo to a duel and Eugeo hit him back, he's still messing around with this shady stuff? You'd better whoop him for good next time."

"I'm telling you, I didn't 'hit him back.' But it's possible that that might have set him off…" Eugeo wondered, biting his lip guiltily. He looked at the girls and explained, "The truth is, I had a duel with Disciple Humbert in the training hall a few days ago. It came out as a draw, but Humbert didn't seem ready to accept that…So it's possible that his recent abuse of Frenica is related…"

"So just because he couldn't beat you, he took it out on his innocent page? The guy doesn't deserve to call himself a swordsman," Kirito spat. The girls still seemed not to understand the full importance of the situation.

Her brow furrowed, Tiese murmured, "So, um…Elite Disciple Zizek challenged Eugeo to a duel, which ended as a draw, and…"

She came to a stop, and Ronie hesitantly finished. "He's… taking it out on her, you said?"

"R-right, that's what I meant. So because he couldn't win, he's using his disciplinary punishment on Frenica out of frustration and forcing her to fulfill his humiliating orders…?"

Despite both being nobles, the girls were the lowest rank and thus the closest to commoners, and they were finding it quite hard to understand the second seat's depraved actions. The thought was so alien to them that they were having difficulty even putting it into words.

Having grown up in a distant rural village, Eugeo could only guess at what Humbert was thinking, and he certainly couldn't identify with it. Sure, Zink had played lots of pranks on him as a kid, but his motive had been very simple: Zink liked Alice and didn't care for the fact that she spent most of her time with Eugeo, so he would hide his rival's shoes.

But Humbert was unleashing his frustration and shame at not winning the duel on his page, who bore no fault in the matter. In fact, he was sworn by his position to offer Frenica friendly advice and instruction.

Eugeo knew about the phrase *temper tantrum*. When he was young, his father had given his eldest brother a wooden sword from the school, and Eugeo was so jealous that he took his own sword, one his father whittled himself, and struck it against a rock outside so hard that it broke. His father explained that this was a temper tantrum, an act of misplaced anger, and was something to be ashamed of. After a good scolding, Eugeo never did such a thing again.

Just like breaking one's own sword, being overly strict on a trainee page was likely not in violation of the Taboo Index, Basic Imperial Law, or even the academy rules. But did that mean it was really *okay* to do it? Could there be other things outside of the written laws, very important things that ought to be followed...?

As Eugeo and the girls grappled with this weighty question, Tiese spoke up to say, "I...I don't understand."

She raised her head and looked right at Eugeo, the youthful noble heir's cheeks extruding over her clenched teeth. "My father always told me that the Schtrinen family's claim to nobility came from some minor feat achieved by a distant ancestor, briefly earning him the attention of the emperor at the time. And because of that, we shouldn't take it for granted that we live in a larger house and have more rights than common people. He says that being a noble means that when the battle finally comes, we stand with our swords at the front and die first, so that the commoners below can live in peace and stability..."

Tiese moved her maple-red eyes south—to the heart of Centoria. She looked at the imposing outline of the imperial government building, just barely visible above the trees, then turned back to Eugeo.

"The Zizeks, meanwhile, have a huge mansion in District Four and their own holdings outside Centoria. So doesn't that mean Elite Disciple Humbert should be working even harder than the lower nobles for the happiness of all? Even if it's not written in the Taboo Index, a noble should always consider if his actions will cause misfortune to others, Father said. Humbert might not be breaking the Taboo Index or the school rules...but...but Frenica cried herself to sleep last night. How...how can such a thing be allowed?"

When she finished her long, impassioned speech, there were large drops in Tiese's eyes. But Eugeo had no answer for her—he'd been grappling with the same question. Ronie extended a white kerchief to Tiese, who put it to her eyes.

"Your father's a great man. I'd like to meet him someday."

That was Kirito, his voice calm and even. It took Eugeo a while to believe what he just heard. The swordsman dressed in black, routinely feared and shunned by his schoolmates for his dangerous glare, blunt attitude, and legendary duel with Volo Levantein, was treating Tiese with sympathy and kindness.

"What your father taught you, Tiese, is what's called in Eng...I mean, in the sacred tongue, the 'noblesse oblige.' It's an idea that the noble, or the powerful, should use that power for the sake of the powerless...It's a kind of pride, in a way."

Despite an entire year's worth of lessons in the sacred tongue, Eugeo had never heard this phrase before, but for some reason, the definition fit squarely into his mind. It made perfect sense.

Kirito's quiet voice rode the spring breeze. "That pride is more important than any laws or rules. There are things that aren't

illegal but should never be done, and sometimes there are things that must be done, even when they are forbidden by law."

In a way, the latter half of that statement was a refutation of the Taboo Index—and the Axiom Church as a whole. Tiese and Ronie gasped. But Kirito fixed his unwavering stare on them and continued, "A long, long time ago, there was a great man named Saint Augustine. He said that an unjust law is no law at all. You must not put blind faith in any law or authority, no matter how powerful. Humbert might not be breaking the Index or school rules, but his actions are wrong. He must not be allowed to bring an innocent girl to tears. That means someone has to make him stop, and if anyone here is going to do that..."

"Right...that's us," Eugeo agreed. "But Kirito...who decides if the law is just or unjust? If everyone decides for him- or herself, then what becomes of the proper order? Isn't that why the Axiom Church exists, to decide that for everyone?"

The Taboo Index did not determine the legality of every single human action. That was how Humbert got away with unfairly punishing his page. But just as Sister Azalia had scolded Zink for his pranks, Eugeo and Kirito had the right to call out Humbert's actions as his classmates. That was a completely separate principle from casting doubt on the structure of the Church itself.

God created the world, and the Church was the holy agent. It had guided humanity correctly for centuries. It could not possibly be wrong.

To his surprise, it was not Kirito who answered this question but the previously silent Ronie. The quiet, shy girl spoke with a force of will that took Eugeo aback.

"Um...I think I know what Kirito means. It's an important mentality that isn't mentioned in the Taboo Index—meaning that it's a type of justice that exists within ourselves. Not to blindly obey the law but to consult the law in accordance with our justice and think about why it exists. Maybe he's saying that it's more important to think than to obey..."

"Exactly, Ronie. The mind is the most powerful tool a human being wields. It's stronger than any sword or secret technique," Kirito replied, grinning. There was admiration in his eyes, and something deeper lurked behind it. Even after two years of constant companionship, there were still things about Kirito that Eugeo didn't know.

He asked, "But Kirito, who was this…Saint Augus-whatever person? An Integrity Knight?"

"Hmm, more like a priest, I bet. Probably long dead," Kirito said, smirking.

Once Ronie and Tiese had headed back to the primary trainee dorm, empty picnic basket in one hand and the other waving good-bye, Eugeo turned to look at his partner.

"About Humbert…do you have a plan, Kirito?"

Kirito frowned and mumbled, "Hmm…something tells me that just commanding him to stop picking on the underclassman isn't going to work. But on the other hand…"

"On the other hand…what?"

"Humbert's one thing, but his boss, Raios, is nasty, scheming, *and* smart. He came out as first seat, so he has to have good marks in sacred arts, law, and history, too."

"True. Better than whoever ended up in sixth seat."

"You can say that about more than one of us," Kirito shot back.

They were on the verge of getting into one of their usual sniping wars, but Eugeo knew it was too important of a topic to get derailed. "And…?"

"Raios shares a common room with Humbert, right? Don't you find it strange that he would just sit back and allow this bullying to happen? Whether he suffers discipline or not, eventually bad rumors are going to get out, and that will affect the reputation of his roommate. That seems like just as much of a stain on Raios's honor as any punishment…"

"Still, it's a fact that Humbert is tormenting Frenica. Doesn't that mean Humbert's so upset that not even Raios can rein him in? If that's stemming from our duel, then I have a responsibility to say something..."

"There. That's it," Kirito said, scowling as if he'd bitten a dried tanglevine. "What if this is their clever trap designed to ensnare you? What if you protest Humbert's actions, and they've set up some kind of trick that will cause you to break the school rules...?"

"What?" Eugeo asked, stunned. "You can't be serious. That's not possible. Humbert and I are still disciples. As long as I don't openly insult him, warnings and admonishment don't count as acts of rudeness. I'm more worried about *you*, Kirito."

"Ah, well...good point. I'd hate to accidentally splash mud on his uniform," Kirito said, straight-faced. Eugeo sighed. At the end of the previous school year, Kirito committed that very act of rudeness against First Seat Volo and had to undergo the punishment of a first-strike duel with real, live blades.

"Listen, when we go to Humbert's room, I'll talk first, got it? You just stand behind me and look menacing."

"Sure thing, boss. I'm good at that."

"...Please, Kirito. We'll try to be diplomatic this time, and if they don't respond to reason, we can petition the management to change Frenica's placement. They'll at least ask Humbert what he's getting up to, and that alone should have an effect on him."

"Yeah...good point," Kirito said, still looking a bit glum. Eugeo slapped him on the back and started walking up the hill to the elite disciple dorm. The righteous fury he felt over Tiese's story stuck with him, quickening his pace.

A year ago today, when he was a newly assigned page with no idea what he was doing, he climbed this hill to visit Golgorosso Balto, an imposing disciple who looked to be in his twenties.

With Golgorosso's massive body, covered in rippling muscles, and sideburns that bristled proudly like the mane of the lions said to live in the southern empire, Eugeo had initially been afraid that he'd wandered into an instructor's room by mistake.

Golgorosso gave the nervous Eugeo a single glance and ordered him to take off his clothes. That was shocking, but Eugeo wasn't going to disobey, so he stripped off his gray uniform and stood there in his underwear. He'd felt the piercing gaze scan him from head to toe—and then Golgorosso smiled at last and said, "You're in good shape."

Eugeo had put the uniform back on with utter relief, and Golgorosso admitted that as a common-born man who rose through the garrison ranks himself, he had chosen Eugeo for his background. In the year that followed, his boldness was sometimes troubling but never crossed the line, and he taught Eugeo much about the sword in his own bracing way. Eugeo's success at the disciple placement tests had as much to do with Golgorosso's Baltio style as it did with Kirito's Aincrad one.

On the day Golgorosso graduated and left the city, Eugeo summoned his courage and asked him the question that had been on his mind all year: Why did he pick Eugeo and not Kirito, who had come up from the same place?

True, I could tell during the entrance tests that his skill was a bit above yours. But that's exactly why I chose you. I could sense that you had further to go and were more desperate to improve yourself, just the way I was. But either way, Liena was second seat, so she got to pick Kirito first.

Golgorosso boomed with laughter and rubbed Eugeo's head with his thick hand. *Earn your way to being a disciple, and treat your page well*, he said. Eugeo nodded repeatedly, fighting back the tears, and stood at the school gate until Golgorosso's imposing form was out of sight.

He had taught Eugeo that a disciple and page were not just a simple instructor and servant. He didn't think he would ever be as good a tutor as Golgorosso was, but he was going to spend this entire year teaching Tiese as much of what he'd learned as possible. Wouldn't that be what Kirito had talked about—something not written in the rules but more important than anything?

Humbert and Raios might not understand it. They'd probably

slacked off in the entrance exams to come in under the top twelve so that they didn't have to be pages. But even so, he had to say what needed to be said.

Eugeo put his hands on the door, pushed his way into the dorm building, and headed up the front stairs, leather boots ringing against every step.

3

He knocked on the eastern door of the third floor, and after a few moments, Humbert's voice asked who was there.

"It's Disciple Eugeo and Disciple Kirito. We'd like to speak with Disciple Zizek," he replied, trying not to sound too aggressive. The sound of rough footsteps came from beyond the door, then it hurtled open. Humbert glared at them and shouted loud enough for anyone down on the ground level to hear:

"It is rude of you to call without a prior arrangement! Your first course of action should obviously have been to put your request for a meeting into writing!"

Before Eugeo could answer, Raios Antinous's soothing voice came from farther in the room. "There, there. They are our fellow pupils and residents. Let them through, Humbert—though I'm afraid we cannot arrange for tea on such short notice."

"...You'd better be grateful for Raios's generous nature," Humbert snarled under his breath, then turned back from the doorway. Eugeo gave them a proper salute and walked inside, wondering what that little bit of theater was all about.

"What in the—?" Kirito started to say as he followed Eugeo in, so the other boy had to loudly clear his throat to drown him out.

They proceeded to the couch in the middle of the room. The room was the same size as theirs, of course, but the internal decorations, from the rugs on the floor to the delicate window drapes rustling in the breeze, were of the highest quality.

Humbert sank into the right end of the couch, which was about three mels long, silk-bound, and stuffed with soft cotton. On the left end, Raios had parked his rear on the edge of the cushion, his head back against the headrest and his feet up on the table, such that he was very nearly lying down.

The noble heirs weren't wearing their school uniforms but lounging around in thin robes. Raios's was red, and Humbert's was yellow, both woven from lustrous southern silk and vivid to look upon. The scent of the tea from the cups sitting on the table suggested green tea from the east. Raios picked his up, gave a leisurely sip, then looked at Eugeo at last.

"Now...what brings our friend Disciple Eugeo here to our chamber on this free evening?"

There was another couch on the other side of the table, but neither of them made any motion to invite the two guests to sit. Eugeo considered that to be in his favor and glared down at them from his standing position with as stern an expression as he could muster.

"We've heard some rather unsavory rumors about your behavior, Disciple Zizek. I've come to deliver an anticipatory warning, before you deal a grave blow to our school's reputation."

Humbert's face immediately screwed up to deliver a raging rebuke, but Raios reached out to still him. Raios grinned up at them, his lips surprisingly red. "Is that so...?"

Through the rising steam of the cup in his hand, he continued, "This is both a surprise and a welcome development. It makes me proud to see you concerned with our academy's reputation. However, I cannot for the life of me imagine what these rumors are. I'm ashamed to have to ask for an explanation."

"I've heard that Zizek has been inflicting vulgar instructions upon his own trainee page. Perhaps that sounds familiar to you?"

"How dare you!" shrieked Humbert, rising from the couch.

"You—a miserable frontiersman without a name—*dare* to accuse me, a fourth-rank noble heir, of being *vulgar*?!"

"That will be enough, Humbert," Raios said, waving his hand again to silence his henchman. "We might be from different backgrounds, but we are all students under the same roof now. Here at this school, no statement can be taken as an insult and breach of decorum...but that will be a different story if the tale is found to be without merit or evidence. Where did you hear this bizarre rumor, Eugeo?"

"Let's not waste any of our valuable time, Antinous. You know full well that it is true. We heard the story straight from primary trainees who share a dorm room with Zizek's page."

"Oh? So I take it that Humbert's page has officially enlisted you to argue on her behalf, through an intermediary dormmate?"

"...Well...not exactly..." Eugeo muttered, promptly at a loss. They hadn't heard the story directly from Frenica's lips, so it would be difficult to dig their heels in if faced with charges of false accusation.

But he couldn't turn back now, not with Raios mocking them from his lazy position and Humbert seething with barely contained rage. "So...you deny these charges? You deny that Humbert has been performing untoward acts upon his page, Frenica?"

"Untoward? That's a rather strange term to use, Eugeo. Why not be clearer and state that they are against the school rules?"

"......"

He paused again. The school rules applied only on campus grounds, but to the students, they were just as important as the Taboo Index and Basic Imperial Law—no one would dare break them.

Eugeo knew full well that Humbert hadn't broken the rules, and that was what made this so despicable. He was doing whatever he knew he could get away with. Eugeo took a deep breath to settle his nerves and said, "But...but even if it's not against the school rules, there are actions that are clearly inappropriate for an upperclassman—especially an elite disciple charged with guiding and tutoring a primary trainee!"

"I see. And what is it that you are accusing Humbert of doing to Frenica, Eugeo?"

"…W-well…"

Eugeo couldn't answer that question. He hadn't wanted to press Tiese and Ronie for details, so he didn't know the exact nature of the "untoward orders." Raios spread his arms theatrically and shook his head from side to side.

"Good grief! This is starting to get ridiculous, I'm afraid. Humbert, do you have any idea what Eugeo is talking about?" he asked. The other man, who'd been leaning forward and staring daggers at Eugeo, threw himself back onto the couch.

"Not in the least! I have no clue what he is referring to! For one thing, I've never done a single vulgar thing to Frenica in my life. She's certainly never said 'no' to anything I've told her to do!" Humbert reached up and slicked back his gray hair, putting on a venomous smile. "At worst, I've only ordered her to provide a few trifling services. As I'm sure you remember, Eugeo, after my miserable draw in our duel the other day, I've been putting myself through harder training than ever before. I used to avoid exercises that added unsightly muscles, but no longer—and my body has been screaming at me for it. So I merely had her massage my sore flesh during my evening baths. And to save her the trouble of a wet uniform, I've been nice enough to allow her to perform the task in her undergarments. I fail to see what makes any of this *vulgar!*"

As Eugeo watched Humbert chuckle delightedly, he sensed an unfamiliar emotion surging up from deep inside him.

Was there any point in politely attempting to convince such a person?

Was it really words that were appropriate now, or a striking blow with a wooden sword?

Eugeo's hand twitched, preparing to draw his practice blade and declare a duel on the spot, but then he realized he had not brought his weapon. He inhaled and exhaled several times, and with as level a voice as he could manage, said, "Humbert, do you think...you will get away with this? There might be no rule against demanding that of her—but only because it should not be necessary to point it out. Ordering your page to disrobe before you is utterly shameless—"

"Ha-ha-ha! Ha-ha-ha-ha-ha!"

Raios abruptly broke the silence, glee on his face. It was as if he'd been waiting for Eugeo to say exactly those words.

"Ha-ha-ha! I never thought I'd hear those words from Disciple Eugeo's mouth! Ha-ha-ha-ha! Especially given that when he was a page, that common-born giant of a man had him remove his uniform every night!"

"Why, what a curious tale! The man who happily stripped to his skin accuses others of being shameless for the same action! Ha-ha!" laughed Humbert, joining in.

Eugeo felt his body tremble again with that unfamiliar urge. He was about to launch an insult that would surely get him into hot water with the school rules when Kirito loudly clicked his heels, bringing him to his senses.

Golgorosso had indeed ordered Eugeo to take off his shirt once or twice a month. But that was only to inspect his musculature and provide more detailed instructions for exercise, nothing more salacious than that. But if he argued to that effect, it would only embolden them, and they'd start insulting Golgorosso, too. So he did his best to hold in the emotion and spoke in a quiet, suppressed voice.

"My experiences are not the point here. All I know is that your page is undergoing great stress because she cannot refuse your orders. If her situation does not improve, I may be forced to petition a teacher to look into the matter. Keep that in mind."

Eugeo turned and left the room, while the other boys laughed and urged him to go ahead with his plan. Once the door had shut behind him, he clenched his fist, ready to smash it against the wall—but he knew he had enough strength to put a dent in it, thus damaging the life of the building. Intentionally destroying school facilities or property clearly violated the rules and would be an example of that "temper tantrum" he'd been warned about. For a moment, he wished for that Gigas Cedar again, its bark so tough that he could smash all his frustration into it without consequence.

As a pathetic replacement, he stomped as hard as he could toward his own room on the west end, when Kirito said, "You need to calm down, Eugeo."

The sound of that familiar voice cooled the burning-red furnace of his mind ever so slightly. Eugeo exhaled. He slowed down so that his partner could catch up.

"I'm...surprised. I figured that you'd explode before I did," Eugeo noted.

Kirito smirked and tapped his waist. "If we had our swords, it would have ben a different story. But like I said earlier, I felt like they were up to something, so I held it in and watched them closely."

"That's right, I remember you saying that. Well, *now* I do...So what did you notice?"

"Humbert is one thing, but I can say for certain that Raios was testing you. He probably figured that you'd heard about Frenica from Tiese and Ronie and was prepared to level the highest possible disciplinary punishment if you crossed a line with Humbert. You really can't underestimate the wicked cunning of the upper nobility..."

"You mean...you think Raios let Humbert carry on because he wanted me to come and argue about it? This is...crazy," Eugeo mumbled, coming to a stop in the middle of the hallway. "And it all starts with my embarrassing Humbert in that duel. How many times did you warn me that nothing good comes from taking their bait...?"

"Don't be too hard on yourself," Kirito said, putting a hand on Eugeo's shoulder in a rare display of tenderness. "We've got the first testing matches coming up. You need to beat them to be the school representative anyway, so you were bound to run afoul of them at some point. I'm guessing that they're satisfied with this for now. Just make sure that the papers to request the faculty's involvement are all prepared, in case we hear that Humbert's still harassing Frenica."

"Yeah...good idea. But if it came to that, I'd have had better luck just breaking down and crying in front of him," Eugeo said, patting Kirito's hand with gratitude. He felt the tension leave his shoulders.

Humbert and Raios were both skilled swordsmen with good scholastic marks as well. They got healthy allowances of *shia* coins from home each month, good for all the clothes or items they could want, and if they got tired of the cafeteria food, they could easily eat out at a restaurant every night. Eugeo couldn't help but be jealous, given how he was making ends meet with his savings from the Zakkaria garrison.

So why did they single out Eugeo at every opportunity, mocking him and attempting to dominate him? What did they think this was getting them? Eugeo knew there were good and bad people in the world, but whether noble or common, they were still human beings, weren't they?

The Axiom Church taught that "good" was the province of the human realm, which was created by Stacia, while "evil" belonged to the Dark Territory ruled by Vecta. That meant that no matter the personality, every human being possessed a heart that was essentially good—even Raios and Humbert.

If they crossed swords in a proper, official match, not one born of a grudge, and exhibited their techniques and skill to their utmost ability, surely they would find some common ground of mutual appreciation. Surely.

Eugeo opened the door to his room and went inside. Before his partner could disappear, he made sure to announce, "Kirito, now that the sacred arts test is done, you're going to practice with me all day tomorrow!"

"You're not usually this excited about it."

"Maybe not…but I've got to get way, way stronger. Raios and Humbert need to know that they can't just sit back without practicing and expect to win every time."

Kirito smirked and nodded. "In that case, I must impress the hardships of training upon Disciple Eugeo."

"That's what I was hoping to hear. Well…see you at dinner."

They waved to each other and retreated to their rooms to change clothes, but Kirito paused halfway, his expression serious. "Be careful, Eugeo. You don't want to get heated if they say something to you when I'm not around."

"I—I know! *Stay cool*, right?" Eugeo said, remembering that the sacred language phrase was both a calming reminder and a parting statement. Kirito smiled in embarrassment for some reason, and then repeated it back to him.

Perhaps they had been satisfied with their triumph, because, during the morning lessons and afternoon classes, Raios and Humbert paid no attention to Eugeo whatsoever. Until last week, Humbert had scowled with hatred every time he saw Eugeo, but now he just looked right past him.

This came as no small relief to Eugeo, of course, but the real issue was whether Frenica's treatment had improved. He and Kirito had filled out and signed the investigation request for the school faculty last night. Once submitted, Raios and Humbert and their pages would be subject to questioning, and they would hate even the suggestion of any slight to their honor.

After the boring imperial history class—in which nothing of incident happened—Kirito went to the library to return a book, and Eugeo headed straight back to the disciples' dorm to wait for Tiese and Ronie.

A short while later, the four o'clock bells rang and the girls showed up, greeting him with good cheer and getting down to the cleaning. Eugeo sat in his chair and watched Tiese tenderly as she worked.

He'd offered a number of times before to help her, but she

always sternly told him that cleaning was part of her duty. With chagrin, he recalled that he'd said something like that to Golgorosso, too. Eugeo tried not to mess up his own room too much in the meantime, but she actually expressed displeasure at that, too—she needed a certain amount of clutter to make the chore worthwhile.

After thirty minutes of twirling around with the long-handled rag, Tiese was done with the common room and bedroom. She entered Eugeo's room, closed the door behind her, and clicked her boot heels.

"Elite Disciple Eugeo, I have a report to make! Today's cleaning has been completed!"

Kirito must have come back, too, as he could faintly hear Ronie's voice through the door. Eugeo decided that his partner could be responsible for explaining the situation to her, so he returned the salute to Tiese and said, "Thanks for the good work, as always."

"No, not at all. This is the page's duty!" she replied, as always. He had to fight not to grin.

"Well, um…I need to talk with you now. Go ahead and take a seat," he said, and then realized that the room had only the one desk chair. If he motioned toward it, she would claim that she'd rather stand, so he headed her off by pointing at the bed by the window.

Tiese's eyes bulged briefly, then she nodded, blushing. "W-well… if you insist."

She walked over and sat timidly on the corner of the bed. Eugeo had to consult his memory to be certain that sitting on a bed with a girl was not against the Taboo Index or the school rules before he took a seat a comfortable distance away. He turned his upper half toward her and put on as serious a face as he could manage.

"About Frenica…I went to confront Humbert about it yesterday. I don't think he wants things to get ugly, so I doubt he'll be making any more of those unreasonable orders. I'll try my best to make him apologize for his actions, too…"

"Oh, I see! That's wonderful...Thank you, Elite Disciple. I'm sure Frenica will be happy," Tiese said, her face shining.

Eugeo answered with a pained smile. "Just call me Eugeo after you're done with your duties. Plus...I owe you an apology. As I tried to explain yesterday, this whole string of events started with my duel with Humbert. When I went to confront him, I realized it was all a plot to inflict disciplinary punishment on *me* for making rude accusations...In other words, Frenica was just collateral damage for Humbert's rivalry with me. I want to meet with her to apologize in person. Do you think you can arrange that...?"

"Oh...I—I see..."

Tiese lowered her head, thinking hard. When she looked back at Eugeo, she shook her head. "No, Eli...Eugeo. It's not your fault. I'll tell her what you said. Um...do you mind if I come a bit closer?"

"Uh...o-okay," Eugeo said, feeling a bit flustered.

Tiese leaned toward him, cheeks much redder now, and shifted closer until he could practically feel her body heat. Then she stared straight ahead at the wall and whispered, "Eugeo, I was thinking really hard last night before I fell asleep, trying to figure out why Elite Disciple Zizek would do such awful things to Frenica, when he couldn't possibly hate her or have some grudge against her... Kirito said that nobles should have pride. But...as a matter of fact, I know that among the higher nobles, there are some who...who toy with the women who live on their property..."

She glanced over at him now, with those eyes the color of an autumnal forest after a long rain.

"I'm...scared. Not long after I graduate, I'll take over the Schtrinen house and end up wedded to another family in the same rank, or perhaps one higher. What if my future husband is...is someone like Zizek? What if he doesn't have that noble pride and he does horrible things to those around him? It's...it's terrifying..."

Eugeo held his breath as he gazed into her teary eyes.

He understood how she felt, but it was also impossible not to be aware of the difference in social class between them. She was Tiese Schtrinen, the eldest child of a sixth-rank noble family, and he was just plain Eugeo, the third son of a pioneer farmer.

Because the harvests in little villages like Rulid were limited, the population had to be carefully managed. Almost without exception, it was the eldest son who took over the house and fields, so (depending on their callings) the later sons were typically forbidden to marry and were bachelors into old age. If he hadn't met Kirito, Eugeo quite possibly could have led a life of nothing more than chopping at the Gigas Cedar every single day. Just like Old Man Garitta.

Now he was living in Centoria among nobles of every stripe—but what would he do if he failed to be school representative after graduating? He could try to get a position within the Imperial Knights or a garrison in some other large town. He could even go all the way back to Rulid to work for his brother. In any case, he'd never need to concern himself with a noble estate.

So naturally, Eugeo was shocked to breathlessness when Tiese leaned over and clung to his arm.

"Uh…Tiese…?!"

The noble girl stared right into Eugeo's bulging eyes from point-blank distance. Her gray uniform gave off a faint scent of solbe leaves.

"Eugeo…I, um…I want to ask you for something. Please, please graduate top of the class, and win the Battle Tournament, and appear in the Four-Empire Unification Tournament."

"Um…well…that's what I'm hoping to do…"

"And then…um…" she said, trying to find the words, her face as red as her hair now. "I-I've heard that if you place highly in the Unification tourney, you can earn a noble title, like Miss Azurica at the primary trainee dorm. So, um…Oh, geez, I really shouldn't be asking you this…but…if you don't end up as an Integrity Knight…will you…will you be my…?"

She couldn't finish that sentence. She just stared at the ground and trembled. Eugeo stared at her petite head, dumbfounded.

It took a little while for him to recognize what she was asking. With understanding came a tiny echo of his own voice inside his head.

The reason I'm trying to get to the Unification Tournament is to be an Integrity Knight and find Alice. That's all. That's all…

But he couldn't explain that to Tiese now. He would lie to her if necessary—she was a sixteen-year-old girl fearing the uncertainty of her future for probably the first time in her life. Yet he could sense that spurning his page's desires at this moment wasn't the right thing to do.

Eugeo lifted his left hand and awkwardly rubbed her head. "Yeah…I know. When the tournament's over, I'll come see you."

Tiese's shoulders quivered, and she slowly, timidly looked up. Tears glistened on her cheeks, and she wore a smile like the budding of spring. "I…I'll get stronger, too. Strong enough to be like you…and say the right things when they need to be said."

4

When the sun dawned on the twenty-second day of the fifth month, they had the first instance of rough weather that spring.

Large drops lashed the windows, hurled by the occasional gust of wind. Eugeo paused from his sword polishing to consider the gray sky—which was already losing Solus's light, despite it being only the end of class.

The layers of dark clouds writhed like some living creature, blasts of purple lightning sneaking through the gaps here and there. Back in Rulid, spring storms were a bane on the villagers, as they would flatten or uproot the fragile young stalks. When Alice had learned the sacred art of weather forecasting, it practically set off a festival celebration. Sadly, they had only two years to make use of that gift before...

It wasn't until he started learning sacred arts at the academy that Eugeo truly understood the immensity of Alice's talent for them. Spells that made use of the laws of nature like weather and geography were some of the most notable higher arts, whose chants could extend over a hundred lines, and Eugeo couldn't even predict if the next day's weather would be sunny or cloudy. Alice had been able to predict the coming of a storm a week ahead of time; by now, she had to be able to manipulate the weather itself. Perhaps this angry storm was a manifestation of her own irritation that Eugeo still hadn't come to get her...

"Ahhh!"

He pushed out that frustration with a groan and resumed polishing the cloudy silver of his blade with the oiled rag. He'd never missed his weekly upkeep of the Blue Rose Sword, but since he'd gained admittance into the academy, these were essentially the only times that he pulled it from its sheath. Everyday practice was with a wooden sword, and for the test matches, each student was given an identical sword to ensure fairness. Compared to the divine object in his hands now, those school blades were much lighter and seemed like they might fly out of the handle if he swung hard enough, but he understood that he couldn't go waving around this tremendous blade in case it destroyed someone's iron sword with a single blow.

The only thing I can imagine freely clashing against with this sword is something similar to that, Eugeo thought as he looked up at the black longsword being polished by his partner on the other couch.

The Gigas Cedar had loomed over the south of Rulid for three centuries, and when it fell at last, they broke off its top branch and lugged the lead-heavy thing with them all the way to Centoria—Kirito often joked that they should just plant it on the side of the road. They took it to Sadore, a metalworker and old friend of Garitta's, and it took an entire year for him to fashion it into this sword.

Sadore, who was practically the dictionary definition of *eccentric*, grumbled that the blade had ruined three blackbrick grindstones that were supposed to last a decade, but he didn't charge them, as it was a once-in-a-lifetime piece of work for him.

The finished sword shone with such a deep, rich light that it was impossible to believe it was made out of a tree branch. Kirito had used it in his duel with Volo Levantein two and a half months ago to achieve a draw, but he hadn't taken it out of its sheath since then except to polish it.

Eugeo was starting to think that they'd never have an actual use for these particular swords during their stay at the school. They couldn't be used in official matches, and it was hard to imagine any other students challenging them to a duel using personal weapons.

So if he wanted to fight with the Blue Rose Sword, he needed to be chosen as school representative and earn entry into the Imperial Battle Tournament. That was the whole idea of being here, of course, but he wasn't entirely sure that he could master this heavy sword within a single match—and on such a huge stage, to boot.

Rather than a student, he'd be facing some veteran of the Imperial Knights or a famous sword-bearing line, with an equally impressive blade of his or her own. Fighting with real blades meant that a blow in the wrong spot could put him in the hospital for a month or two.

As a matter of fact, both Volo Levantein and Sortiliena, the last year's school representatives, had fallen to the knighthood's representative. Liena's whip had been sliced and knocked from her hands, but Volo's left shoulder had been crushed and broken. Normal sacred healing arts were enough to seal the skin and prevent the dropping of his life, but it couldn't repair the bone—he was probably still undergoing treatment.

According to the newspaper that was pasted on the bulletin board once a week, that representative of the Imperial Knights was from one of the most elite imperial noble families of all: the first-rank Woolsburg line. He won not only the Battle Tournament but the Four-Empire Unification Tournament in April and was invited to the holy garden of the Axiom Church to be honored.

Perhaps it was no surprise that Liena and Volo would lose to such an opponent—but Eugeo *had* to win, no matter whom he faced. At next year's Unification Tournament, he had to emerge triumphant, like this year's Norlangarth representative, and pass through the gate of Central Cathedral. There was no other choice.

I'll need your help. Please lend it to me, he prayed to his sword as he polished the tip. Meanwhile, Kirito was sliding his blade through the folded rag. Eugeo stared at that pitch-black sword, shining in the lamplight, and said, "Hey, Kirito."

"What?"

"Have you come up with a name for your sword yet?"

It was the fourth time he'd asked since the sword was finished, and the answer Kirito gave him was again the same: "Erm... nope..."

"Just name the damn thing already. You can't keep calling the poor sword 'the black one' forever."

"Hmm...well, at the place I used to live, the swords' names kind of came with them...um, I think," Kirito mumbled vaguely. Eugeo was going to tear into him again when Kirito's hand shot up all of a sudden.

"Wh-what?"

"Hang on. Was that the four-thirty bell?"

"Uh..."

Eugeo paused and listened. Through the howling of the wind, he could hear the faint sound of bells ringing.

"You're right. That late already? I didn't even hear the four o'clock chime," Eugeo muttered, looking out of the darkened window.

But Kirito's expression was hard. "Ronie and Tiese are late."

Eugeo's breath caught in his throat. Tiese and Ronie hadn't shown up later than four o'clock to clean their rooms once. Eugeo shrugged, trying to fight back the creeping sense of worry.

"Well, the storm's pretty bad. Maybe they're just waiting until the rain stops. It's not like there's a rule about when they have to start..."

"Do you think rain would keep them away...?" Kirito asked, looking at his hands in thought. "I've got a bad feeling about this. I'm going down to the primary trainee dorm. You wait here, just in case I miss them by accident."

He slid his black sword into its sheath, placed it on the table, and got up. There was a light rain jacket nearby that he fastened with his left hand while opening the window with his right.

Eugeo screwed up his face against the burst of wind and rain and said, "Um, Kirito, shouldn't you go out the d…"

But his partner had already leaped from the windowsill to a nearby branch and slid down out of sight, leaving only the sound of rustling leaves. Eugeo sighed, exasperated, and shut the window behind him.

With the sounds of the storm at bay, suddenly the burning of the lamp on the wall seemed much louder. Eugeo returned to the couch, picked up his sword, and sheathed it, disquiet steadily building in his chest.

Higher sacred arts could tell you the location of a person, but they required a lot of spatial power and thus a catalyst. And on the school grounds, any arts that targeted another person were forbidden, even if benign. All Eugeo could do was sit on the couch and wait for something to happen.

After several long minutes of nothing, there was a small knock on the door.

Eugeo exhaled a huge breath. *See? Of course you'll miss them if you jump out the window*, he thought, getting off the couch and crossing the room to the door.

"Thank goodness, I was wor—"

The words caught in his throat. It wasn't the familiar red and dark-brown hair he was expecting but a light brown tousled by the wind.

A strange girl was standing in the hallway, neither Ronie nor Tiese. Her short hair and gray primary uniform were wet from the rain, and her dripping cheeks were pale. Her large, doe-like eyes were full of impatience and panic, and her lips were trembling.

In a quavering voice, she said, "Um…are you Elite Disciple Eugeo…?"

"Uh…y-yes. Who are you…?"

"I...I'm Frenica Cesky. I-I'm sorry for visiting you without making arrangements first. B-but...I just don't know what to do..."

"Oh...you're Frenica?"

He gave the short girl another examination. She had a delicate body that seemed ill-suited to swordplay and tiny hands that looked more like they were meant to weave crowns of flowers. His rage at Humbert rose anew.

But before he could say anything else, Frenica clutched her hands to her chest and pleaded, "Um...Disciple Eugeo, I'm so grateful to you for what you've done about Humbert Zizek and me. I'll spare you the details of what's happened to me, as I'm sure you already know. But...tonight, he ordered me to perform some tasks that are...d-difficult to explain here..."

Her face was deathly pale and tense, and Eugeo could sense that the shame of those words had to be burning her alive on the inside.

"I...I admitted to Tiese and Ronie that if I had to keep following those instructions, I...I'd rather quit the academy. Instead, they rushed off to plead to him in person..."

"What?" he rasped. He felt his fingers gripping the white leather scabbard going cold.

"But I just kept waiting, and they never came back, and I...I just don't know what to—"

"When did they leave?"

"Um, I think it was right after the three-thirty bell."

That was over an hour ago. Eugeo held his breath, looking across the hallway toward the far door. The girls had been here, on the third floor of the disciples' dorm, this whole time. That was far too much time for an argument or petition.

He turned back to the storm-beaten window, but Kirito was not about to return through it. It would take at least fifteen minutes to visit the primary trainee dorm and come back in this weather. There was no time to wait around.

"All right," he said to Frenica quickly. "I'll go check it out. You wait here in this room. And…if Kirito shows up, tell him to come to Humbert's room, will you?"

She nodded uncertainly, and Eugeo left the room. After a few steps down the parquet hallway, he realized he was still holding the Blue Rose Sword, but he didn't want to turn around to put it back. He let it hang in his left hand and walked east down the curving hallway. With each step, the mass of anxiety in his chest grew.

The reason the girls had gone to argue their case directly was clear. Eugeo and Kirito's first argument had not been successful, and Tiese had admitted her wish to him the night before—she wanted the strength to say the right thing, and now she had a chance to test that resolve.

But perhaps…that was…

"Was that the intent from the very start…? Not us but the girls…?" he muttered under his breath as he ran.

Between trainees and disciples of the same rank, you could speak freely without problems. But a primary trainee and an elite disciple was a different matter. They'd have to choose their words very carefully to avoid breaking the school rule on politeness. If they crossed the line, the disciple could choose to enforce disciplinary punishment in the place of a faculty member. Kirito had learned this lesson the hard way with Volo Levantein.

Eugeo consulted his memory of the school rules.

When an elite disciple hands down disciplinary punishment, one of the following three types of commands is allowed. 1) Cleaning the school grounds (see area limits). 2) Training with a wooden sword (see regimen). 3) A duel with the disciple (see rules). In all cases, higher law takes priority.

"Higher law" meant Basic Imperial Law and the Taboo Index, of course. In other words, the taboo against reducing the life of another without reason still held priority over the disciplinary punishment. If Humbert commanded Tiese and Ronie to accept a duel and insisted it be first-blow rather than stop-short, he would not be allowed to physically harm them if they did not accept. So there shouldn't be too much to fear about Humbert's punishment.

But the worry and dread that stabbed at his heart would not abate.

At the east end of the circular third-floor hallway, the door was closed. Eugeo didn't even wait to gather his breath. He slammed his fist against it.

After a few seconds, Humbert's muffled voice answered. "Well, well, you're late to arrive, Elite Disciple Eugeo. Please, do come in and grace us with your presence!"

It was as if he'd been waiting for Eugeo to come, a realization that only quickened his pulse. He yanked the door open.

The fancy lamps they'd installed were dimmed, making the shared common room much darker than the last time he'd been here. There was some thick eastern incense burning, hazing the air in the room. Eugeo grimaced at the smell, looking around.

At the couches in the center, wearing the same thin robes as yesterday, were Raios and Humbert. Raios sat with his back to Eugeo, legs up on the table again, glass in his left hand. The contents were dark red, probably wine. Alcohol was allowed in the disciples' dorm, with certain restrictions, but drinking on a normal day was frowned upon.

Across from him, Humbert was clearly intoxicated already. There was a slack smile on his reddened face as he leered, "Don't just stand there. Come here and sit, Eugeo. We just opened a fifty-year vintage from the western empire. Common folks rarely get a chance to sample such fine drink!"

So Humbert wasn't just offering him a seat but a drink as well. Eugeo silently looked around the room, feeling even stranger. Gloomy though the room was, he could see no one else was there.

Had Ronie and Tiese already left? Had they even been here? If they'd come and gone, why didn't they at least stop at Kirito and Eugeo's room on the other end of the hall? Questions raced through Eugeo's brain, but the girls' absence did at least remove some tension from his shoulders.

"No, I don't drink alcohol. More importantly, Disciple Zizek," he said, moving forward and choosing his words carefully, "did you perhaps have a visit today from my page, Tiese Schtrinen, or Disciple Kirito's page, Ronie Arabel?"

It was not Humbert who answered him but Raios Antinous. He looked over his shoulder, still holding up the glass, eyes narrowed.

"...Disciple Eugeo, you look pale to me. Why not take a glass to revive your spirits?"

"No, thank you. Will you answer my question?"

"Hah, what a shame. I'm only thinking of you—as a friend."

Eugeo could sense the slick sweat in the palm of his hand as it gripped the sword sheath. Raios gazed at him like he was a snack to go with his drink, took a tiny sip, and set the cup down on the table.

"Ahh. So...those were your pages, were they?" he said easily, licking the moisture from his lips. "They are bold trainees, to pay an unannounced visit to the first and second seats who stand above all other students in this academy. Small wonder they're yours. But you ought to be careful—sometimes boldness can spill into rudeness and disrespect. Don't you agree, Disciple Eugeo? Oops...pardon me. I suppose I'm wasting my time lecturing you on the courtesy of the nobility. Ha-ha, ha-ha-ha..."

So Tiese and Ronie had come here.

Eugeo could barely resist the urge to grab the collar of Raios's robe. His voice was low and tense. "I will hear your lecture on another occasion. Where are Tiese and Ronie now?"

This time it was Humbert who languidly poured more wine and said, "Eugeo...was the burden too much for you to bear? How is a mere lumberjack from the most distant lands supposed to instruct a noble girl, even one of the lowest rank? Ha-ha-ha... you couldn't. You didn't know enough to teach them not to hurl disrespectful accusations at a fourth-rank noble like me. Distasteful as I found it, I had no choice but to fulfill my grand duty. It is the role of the upper nobles to correct the lower."

"Humbert, what did you...?!"

Eugeo stopped short when the man held out his free hand, drained the glass, and got to his feet. Raios stood next and took a few steps farther toward the back of the room. Standing together, the nobles looked like brothers, wearing wicked grins as they shared a glance.

"Well, Raios...shall we have Eugeo indulge in the finest pleasure of the evening?"

"Indeed, Humbert. We're missing one other audience member, but I'm tired of waiting. I'm sure he'll catch up soon."

"Pleasure...? Tired of waiting...?" Eugeo repeated, numb. Humbert jutted out his long jaw, mocking him. The two disciples turned, robes fluttering, and headed to the bedrooms on the west side of the room. Eugeo walked unsteadily after them.

Behind the door Humbert opened, the darkness was absolute, choked with the smoke of incense. Raios walked through first, followed by his partner.

Eugeo stopped when he saw the lavender smoke wisping along the floor. The trail felt like the smoldering of true evil, a thing that should not exist at the academy—should not exist in this vast empire. It was even worse than the smoke of the campfire lit by those wicked goblins in the far northern cave years ago.

His reflexes wanted him to turn away, but something in the smell caught his attention, something clean. A note like the familiar scent of solbe leaves.

The smell from Tiese's uniform.

"...Tiese...Ronie!"

He raced forward into the bedroom just as the lamp came on.

The first thing he saw was a large canopy bed with two girls lying on it. No, *laid upon* it. Both were tied up with bright-red ropes on top of their gray primary trainee uniforms. Their eyes, red and brown, were staring absently into space, their minds apparently dulled by the thick incense fumes.

"Wha...? Wh-why...?"

Eugeo rushed toward the bed to at least untie the ropes first. Then Raios cried, "Not so fast!" and thrust out a palm into his face. Eugeo glanced over at the man and rasped, "Wh-what do you think you're doing, Raios?! Why are our pages being treated like—?"

"This is a necessary measure, Eugeo."

"Necessary...measure...?"

"Indeed. Primary Trainee Schtrinen and Primary Trainee Arabel visited this bedroom without a prior arrangement and displayed brazen disrespect for us."

"What kind...of disrespect?" Eugeo repeated.

Humbert leaned away from the wall, leering. "You should have heard the things they said. You wouldn't believe your ears. Those lesser nobles dared to accuse me of mistreating my page, without reason, to fulfill my own desires—*me*! When I, as second seat of this fine academy, am merely and rightfully guiding Frenica! Even a generous, understanding man such as I could not overlook this slight."

"And that's not all, Eugeo. They also claimed that, as I share a common room with Humbert, I am complicit in the actions they accuse him of committing. And when I said I did not understand...Can you believe it? That sixth-rank noble girl asked me, a third rank myself, if I had no pride as a nobleman! My goodness, what a question."

Humbert and Raios shared a look and chuckled. It was clear now that they'd orchestrated the situation to produce this exact result. Humbert knew that Frenica was close to Tiese and Ronie and intentionally disgraced and humiliated her—until the other girls came directly to argue on her behalf.

The girls would have minced their words at first, of course. But Raios and Humbert were too slippery, too coaxing to keep them on safe footing. Eventually, they would have said something that could be taken as rude and protocol breaking.

…However.

"But Raios, even if this is all true…tying them up and locking them in your room is clearly beyond the bounds of the disciplinary punishment powers we possess!" Eugeo snapped, just barely holding his thunderous emotions in check.

The girls were tied up over their uniforms and didn't seem to be wounded. But the only punishment allowed for acts of rudeness were cleaning, training, and duels. Abduction with restraints did not match any of those options. Raios and Humbert had to be breaking school rules—

"Disciplinary punishment?" Raios murmured, leaning closer to Eugeo. "When did I say that I was making use of that childish, limited power?"

"Wh-what do you mean? The school rules are quite strict in how they define the allowed types of punishment for trainee breach of protocol…"

"That's where you've made your mistake. Have you forgotten *this* part of the school rules? 'In all cases, higher law takes priority.'"

Raios's expression swiftly changed. His red lips curled upward at the ends, turning sadistic to a degree Eugeo had never seen before.

"Higher law means the Taboo Index and Basic Imperial Law. That means I cannot directly damage their life. Those ropes are made of fine eastern silk, very stretchy…They will not harm what they hold, no matter how tightly they are tied."

"B-but…there's no way you can tie up a student for punishment, no matter how fine the ropes are…"

"Don't you get it yet, Disciple Eugeo? If higher law takes precedence, that means it's not disciplinary punishment I'm inflicting on this sixth-rank girl for talking back to a third-rank nobleman…it's my *judicial authority as a noble*!"

Judicial authority.

Eugeo instantly recalled his conversation with Tiese in the forest the other day. Only fourth-rank and higher nobles had the right to wield judicial authority, and the ranks below that were subject to its powers...

Raios waited, clearly savoring the dumbfounded expression on Eugeo's face. After a few moments, he spread his arms theatrically and declared, "Judicial authority is the greatest of noble privileges! It only applies to fifth- and sixth-rank noble families and the common people who live on our private estates, but the contents of the punishment are up to us! We must follow the Taboo Index, of course, but as long as it is not a taboo, we can do *anything*!"

Eugeo recovered from his shock at last. "B-but Raios! Just because you can choose your punishment doesn't make it right to tie up teenage girls like this! It's too cruel..."

"Ha-ha...ha-ha-ha, *ha-ha-ha-ha-ha*!!" Humbert cackled. He doubled over, yellow sleeves flying. "Ha-ha-ha! This is too rich, Raios! Disciple Eugeo thinks that our judicial review is merely to tie them up with ropes!"

"Heh-heh. Can you blame him, Humbert? He's fresh down to the big city from his home up in the hills, and the disciple he served was just as common as he is! But I think after today, Eugeo will finally understand just what sort of power we nobles wield!" Raios said, and turned away.

He strode up to the bed where Tiese and Ronie lay and knelt atop the mattress. The frame creaked, and Tiese blinked blearily.

Then her red eyes bolted open and took account of Raios as he descended upon her. Her frail voice filled the room. "No...no...!"

She twisted, trying to escape, but could do nothing with her limbs bound. Raios extended a pale, clammy hand to trace her cheek. Next to them, Humbert climbed up as well, running his hands along Ronie's legs. She awakened, too, took stock of the situation, and gaped silently.

At last, from barely three mels away, Eugeo understood the nature of this judicial "decision."

Raios and Humbert were going to defile Tiese and Ronie with their own bodies. They were going to forcefully perform the act that Stacia granted only to a husband and wife—or so Eugeo believed—as a means of noble authority.

In the instant of understanding, Eugeo screamed, "Stop!!"

He took a step toward the bed, and Raios bolted upright, his eyes gleaming.

"Stay back, commoner!!" he commanded, pointing at Eugeo with one hand while his other fondled Tiese's face. "This is the just and absolute right of nobility, as ordained by Basic Imperial Law and the Taboo Index! Interference with our judicial authority is a crime in itself! One more step, and you will be a criminal in violation of the law!"

"That's..."

That's not my problem! Get away from Tiese and Ronie! he wanted to shout. He wanted to leap onto Raios as he screamed it.

But suddenly his legs came to a stop, as definitely as if they'd been nailed into the ground. The halt in momentum was so sudden, he fell to his knees. His legs wouldn't cooperate, wouldn't help him stand up again.

Inside his head, the phrase *criminal in violation of the law* repeated over and over. Eugeo didn't care about the law. He didn't care about anything other than helping Tiese and Ronie, but he was subject to the whim of a voice that was not his.

The Axiom Church was absolute. The Taboo Index was absolute. Disobedience was forbidden. It was forbidden to all.

"*Hrgh...gah...!!*"

He gritted his teeth, gasped, and raised his right leg. It felt as though his familiar leather boot—and the foot inside—was as heavy as lead.

Raios watched this display of will and hissed, "That's right. Stay there and watch like a good boy."

"*Rgh...rrrgh...*"

He ignored the taunt, desperately moving that foot back to the ground, but he could do no more. Even now, Raios's filthy hands were reaching for Tiese and Ronie on the bed.

"...Eugeo," came a fragile voice. He moved his eyes, the only part of his body he could control.

With Raios moving to mount her, Tiese had her face turned to look at Eugeo. Those apple-red cheeks were pale with terror, but her eyes shone with a meaningful willpower.

"Don't move, Eugeo. I'll be...fine. I've earned...this punishment," she said, her voice halting. Then she nodded and rolled her face upward again. She glared at Raios in defiance, then shut her eyes. Ronie had her face buried in Tiese's shoulder but was no longer shrieking.

Raios seemed a bit surprised, taken aback at the strength of their will. Then he grinned venomously. "Very impressive resolve for a sixth-rank noble girl. It'll be interesting to see how long they can last, eh, Humbert?"

"Let's see which will break down into tears first, Raios!"

There was no nobility or pride in their actions now. Their faces were full of vulgar excitement and lust.

He'd seen that look before. Through dulled wits focused on moving his stonelike legs, Eugeo tried to remember. Yes—it was the expression the goblins wore back in that cave. They were the spitting image of the denizens of darkness who attacked Kirito and him with their scimitars.

Raios and Humbert reached to touch the girls' faces at the same time, running their fingers down foreheads and cheeks, savoring the fear and humiliation. They deftly avoided touching the girls' lips, as physical contact there—before the kiss that sealed a marriage—was forbidden. But if that was forbidden, how could the law allow this kind of assault on an unmarried woman? What purpose could there be in such a law?

Throb.

A sharp pain jolted deep inside his right eye. The odd, familiar pain from whenever he questioned the law or the Church.

Ordinarily, Eugeo would instinctually stop thinking when he felt it. But this time, this one time, as he crumpled to the floor, Eugeo's mind kept racing.

All the laws and taboos existed to ensure that every resident of the human realm could live in peace and happiness; it had to be so. Thou shalt not steal. Thou shalt not harm. Thou shalt not disobey the Axiom Church. The obedience of the masses was how the world stayed at peace.

But then, why did the many laws only "forbid"? Why create hundreds of pages of rules forbidding this and that, when you could simply write, "All human beings shall respect their fellows, treat them with courtesy, and act with good faith and benevolence"? One simple sentence in the Taboo Index, and these men would never have laid this trap to torture Tiese and Ronie.

Because it was impossible. Even with the absolute authority of the Church, it was impossible for all people to act solely out of goodness. Because…because…

Because all people embody both good and evil.

The Taboo Index was merely suppressing a facet of human evil. That was how Raios and Humbert could easily slip through the loopholes of the law—in fact, to *use* the law to their advantage—to prey upon the innocent like this. And Eugeo had no ability or right to stop them. At the moment, the law allowed them to do this and forbade Eugeo from preventing it.

The nobles had completely forgotten about him by now, their eyes gleaming with lust and power as they surveyed their helpless victims. They undid the front of their robes, growing closer to performing the final act.

Tiese's and Ronie's faces quaked in even greater terror and revulsion as they sensed the men approaching. They shook their heads back and forth in futile resistance, but even that action only added fuel to the predators' enjoyment.

At last, Ronie gave in and begged, "N-no…no…no…!"

Hearing her friend whimper broke down Tiese's last bit of

bravery. Tears spilled onto her cheeks as she wailed, "Please…
help…help, Eugeo! Eugeoooo!"

Tiese and Ronie had summoned all their courage to step up for
the sake of their friend Frenica—and the law blessed this hideous
treatment of them.

Raios and Humbert had plotted and schemed to ensnare
the girls so that they could humiliate them and steal their
chastity—and the law did nothing to stop them.

Was it an act of goodness to uphold this law?

"I…"

With every last ounce of will, Eugeo lifted his leaden body off
the ground, stretching his arm across his side to pull the hilt of
the Blue Rose Sword. The pain in his right eye had transcended
into a lump of burning fire, turning his vision red. He ignored it
and squeezed.

Once he drew the sharp steel sword and turned it on the two
men, Eugeo would lose everything he'd gained at this school—
his fifth-seat position, his enrollment, his dream of being school
representative and appearing in the Imperial Battle Tournament.

But if he stood here and watched as they committed these acts,
he would lose something even more precious—his pride as a
swordsman…and his human heart.

In the woods the other day, Kirito had said there were things
that had to be done, even if they were against the law. Things more
important than the law, than the Index, than the Axiom Church.

It all made sense now.

He knew why Alice had touched the dirt of the land of darkness all those years ago. She had gone to help the dark knight
whose chest the Integrity Knight had pierced. She did that to
protect what was precious inside *her*.

Now it was Eugeo's time. He couldn't put what that precious
thing was into words—in fact, most of the people in the world
might even think of his action as evil.

"But…I have to!" he screamed, the words inaudible. He tried to
pull the sword from its sheath.

Ka-ching.

But it was as though both sword and sheath, and perhaps even his arm itself, had turned to ice. His right arm simply stopped moving. A tremendous jolt of agony shot from his right eye, back to the center of his head. Sparks burst through his bright-red vision. His mind took flight.

...What...is this?

......Actually......it's like back then.

Eight years ago. In the clearing out in front of the church in Rulid. When he tried to stop the Integrity Knight from taking Alice away.

Unable to move, unable to speak, sword a few measly milices loose.

His legs felt rooted deep into the ground, impossible to move even the tiniest bit.

Raios and Humbert sensed something happening and turned to see him humiliatingly frozen in place, hand on his sword. They leered at him, then slowly, theatrically, lowered their waists toward their wailing victims, watching his reaction.

An odd phenomenon then happened between them.

In the center of his right-eye vision, now dyed a pale red, was a shining circle of sacred letters in the color of blood, rotating to the right. It said, SYSTEM ALERT: CODE *871*, but he had no idea what it meant.

But Eugeo could sense that this was some kind of seal. A magical seal placed deep in his eye that prevented him from moving, now and eight years ago, forcing him to comply with the law. This was why he had only been able to stand and watch as Alice was taken away.

"Urgh...hrg...aaah...!"

He desperately clung to his consciousness, trying to prevent it from leaving him altogether as he concentrated on the crimson seal. And on the other side of that vision, the sight of Raios and Humbert, preparing to pierce the bodies of those girls with their own.

It was unforgiveable. Absolutely unforgiveable. He turned that hatred into the strength to move his arm. The blade slid along the sheath. As it did, the sacred letters grew larger and rotated faster.

"N-nooooo! Eugeoooo!!" Tiese screamed.

"Rrraaaahhhh!!" Eugeo roared.

A silver light exploded in his right eye, and the eyeball burst from the inside with a squelching sensation.

Even the loss of half his sight did not register to Eugeo as he yanked on the hilt of the sword. The blade was glowing bright blue, even before it came out all the way—the Aincrad-style secret technique Horizontal.

Raios caught its lightning flash out of the corner of his eye and dipped down just in time. The sword caught his hair as it dropped, slicing the fibers free.

But behind him, Humbert was too slow to react. He halted just before he entered Ronie, swayed left, and then gaped at what he saw.

"Aah..."

A brief shriek was cut short as he raised his left arm in reaction—and the Blue Rose Sword caught it directly on the elbow.

There was no physical feedback. But the blade cut straight through Humbert's left arm, the loose half spinning through the air until it landed on the fine carpet.

No one moved or made a sound. Eugeo paused at the finish of his swing, feeling the pain in his nonexistent right eye.

After an eternity, the raised stump of Humbert's arm sprayed a gush of blood. Most of it landed on the shining sheets, dyeing them red, but some of the liquid landed on Eugeo's left side, spotting his dark-blue uniform.

"Ah...aaah...*aaaaaah*!!"

The guttural shriek burst out of Humbert's throat. His eyes bulged, staring at the blood spurting out of his severed elbow.

"My...my arm...my arm! Blood...all the blood...! My life...my life is draining away!!"

At last he had the presence of mind to squeeze the stump with his remaining hand, but that did not stop the blood. The liquid continued gushing onto the sheet, seeping over toward Raios next to him.

"R-Raios! Sacred arts! No...the normal kind won't work in time! Life...Share your life with me!!" he pleaded, reaching out with his bloodied hand. Raios ducked away from it and got off the bed. Tiese and Ronie were unable to process what had happened and lay on the sheets, expressions blank.

"Raios, give me liiiife!" Humbert wailed, but Raios merely looked at him in surprise and cold impassivity.

"Stop squealing, Humbert. You're not going to lose your life over a single arm...or so the readings suggest. Tie up the wound with that rope to stop the bleeding."

"B-but..."

"More importantly, did you see that, Humbert?"

Humbert was trying to wind the two ropes holding the girls' legs together around his arm now, expression desperate, but Raios turned away to look at Eugeo, who was kneeling at the end of his swing. The nobleman's tongue flicked out and wet his lips.

"That country bumpkin there cut off your arm. It's tremendous, fantastic...I've never seen someone break taboos this way. I was hoping for an act of rudeness at best...and I got a violation of the Taboo Index itself!! Truly fabulous!!"

Raios spun around, his open robe swaying, and walked to the wall on the other side of the bed. He pulled down a large longsword in a red leather scabbard. "Ordinarily, only lower nobles and residents of our holdings are the targets of judicial authority...but certainly that limitation doesn't apply to a taboo-breaking criminal!"

He looked even more excited now than he had when he was about to attack Tiese. Raios drew his sword. It gleamed like a mirror as he held it up with his right hand.

Outside the window, an especially loud blast of thunder sounded. Purple light caught the blade and glinted in Eugeo's left eye. It was clear that Raios Antinous intended to render Eugeo's judgment with that sword—to kill him. But Eugeo couldn't move. Even after violating the Taboo Index, with his right eye blown out by that mysterious seal, he was too shocked to hold up his sword, or even move, after the stunning impact of his attack on Humbert.

"Hah…heh-heh-heh! It's too bad, Disciple Eugeo. I really was looking forward to facing you at next month's testing match. Who could have seen that our parting would come in this manner?" Raios said, his voice lilting with mad joy. He stepped forward. Then again.

Through his blurred left eye, Eugeo saw the sword rise high.

He had to move; he had to avoid his almost certain death. But on the other hand, another voice told him it didn't matter anymore. The dream of being an Integrity Knight and seeing Alice again was dead. His sword had tasted human blood, and he was a criminal. But at least he saved Tiese and Ronie. Neither Raios nor Humbert would try to hurt them anymore. So at least his terrible crime had achieved one meager good.

"Heh, heh-heh…even I have never cut off a man's head with my sword before. I doubt even Father or Uncle has done it. This will make me stronger…far stronger than even that cocky Levantein heir."

Again, Raios's sword and face glowed, followed by another burst of thunder. On the floor, Humbert was cradling his lost arm, but he looked up, briefly forgetting his pain, while, trapped on the bed, Tiese was trying to say something.

Eugeo smiled back at the primary trainee who had worked so hard at being his page for the past month, then hung his head.

"Disciple Eugeo—no, Eugeo the Guilty!! I, Raios Antinous, third-rank noble son, hereby sentence thee to judicial authority!! Give up all of your life to the gods…and do penance for your sin!!" Raios announced. His blade roared.

Gwiiing! A metallic crash. Eugeo waited, but no sword landed on his neck. He raised his head—and saw.

Right in midair, Raios's sword had met another…a pitch-black blade that held it in place. The sleeve around the arm hanging over his head was also black. The intruder's hair, slick with rain—black.

"Kiri...to..." Eugeo mumbled. He'd gone all the way to the primary trainees' dorm to look for the girls, and yet he was here. His partner mouthed the word *Sorry*. Then he stared forward at his opponent.

"Remove your sword, Raios. I won't let you hurt Eugeo."

Raios sneered hatefully as he recognized his foe, but the smile eventually came back. "At last you arrive, Disciple Kirito. But sadly, you are too late! That bumpkin there is no longer even a citizen of the empire, much less a student here. He is guilty of breaking the Taboo Index! I, Raios Antinous, third-rank noble and first-seat elite disciple, have the authority to pass judgment on his crime! So stand back and watch as this criminal's head falls from his shoulders...just as your flowers fell!!"

In contrast to Raios's long and haughty speech, Kirito's response was far shorter and heavier.

"I don't care about your taboos and noble rights."

His eyes gleamed as they stared at Raios. He didn't bother to wipe away the water dripping from his bangs. "Eugeo is my friend. And you are scum, lower than the goblins of the land of darkness."

Shock appeared first on Raios's face, followed by hatred, then a savage joy. "My goodness...What a shock! So both of you hayseeds were agreeable enough to commit treasonous crimes together! Now I can eliminate the both of you. What a glorious day...Truly, Stacia smiles upon me!!"

He pulled back his sword and held it high again. This time, he clutched the handle with both hands and turned sideways, long robes rustling. When he crouched, the blade glowed a blackened red color: the High-Norkia secret technique, Mountain-Splitting Wave.

Without realizing it, Eugeo tried to get to his feet as soon as he saw the stance.

During his duel with Volo Levantein a few months ago, Kirito had bested that same attack with the four-part Aincrad skill Vertical Square. But Raios's attack seemed to swirl with a wicked, twisted energy that he'd not seen before. It wouldn't have the skill that Volo's technique did, but Raios's burgeoning noble pride was feeding it a terrible strength of its own.

Sensing that even Kirito couldn't handle this alone, Eugeo desperately tried to get up, but he could not will any power into his legs.

Suddenly, he felt his partner's hand push on his shoulder. "It's all right," Kirito murmured, moving Eugeo against the wall. Once back in place, he gripped his sword with both hands, like Raios did.

This action stunned Eugeo, even through his quickly fading wits. Like the Zakkarite style, Aincrad style was almost entirely one-handed—and none of the secret arts were two-handed. Besides, both Kirito's sword and the Blue Rose Sword didn't have the handle length for two…

"……!!"

Suddenly, understanding struck, and Eugeo gasped.

The handle of Kirito's black sword grew, emitting little tinging noises. In fact, it wasn't just the handle—the blade itself was expanding in both width and length. Not as big as Raios's massive sword but a good five or six cens longer than Eugeo's.

Kirito held his enlarged black sword above the waist on his right side. It buzzed, vibrating the air, and glowed a jade-green color. That wasn't Aincrad style. It was the Serlut style's Ring Vortex—a move he'd seen at the testing matches last year.

"Kah! Ka-ha-ha…So in your desperation, you turn to mimicking the work of others?! My greatest technique will shatter your measly attempt!!"

"Come on, Raios! You've earned enough debt; now it's time to pay up!!"

Both swords roared with power, lighting the small bedroom in red and green.

Humbert, huddling on the floor in the back; Tiese and Ronie, now sitting up on the bed and clutching each other; and Eugeo, kneeling along the wall—all silently watched the two swordsmen.

It was a fight between elite disciples—a showdown they would have seen at next month's testing match, if not for today's events. The next bolt of lightning was the signal to start.

"*Kyeaaaaa!!*" Raios screamed, and brought his sword down.

"*Seyaa!!*" Kirito belted, slicing upward on a diagonal.

Red and green trails of light clashed in midair, rumbling the floorboards and blowing all the glass windows outward. As he stared at the intersection of the black and silver blades, Eugeo understood why Kirito hadn't used the Aincrad style.

The speedy but light single-handed attacks would not be enough to stop a double-handed High-Norkia technique. It would require leaping away at the moment of impact to disperse the shock, then chaining together more swings after that, but that wasn't possible without the space of the training hall. Maybe in the common room next door, but Kirito had no choice but to fight here to protect Eugeo. That was why he chose to use the Serlut two-handed Ring Vortex.

"K-Kirito!!" Eugeo gasped, his throat parched, right as Kirito fell to his left knee. The black sword was being pushed backward, creaking with the pressure. Raios's eyebrows and the corners of his mouth had risen as high as they could, and he screeched with triumph.

"How's that...? How do you like that?! You miserable, inferior peasants!! Why would you ever think you could get the better of Raios Antinous?! You might be able to bring dead flowers to life with some occult arts, but your parlor tricks will not affect *my* sword!!"

The glow infusing Raios's blade shifted from red to filthy black, spreading from the weapon up his arms and around his body, his robes and golden hair rippling. Kirito's position was pushed back near to his original stance, the green color on his sword flickering weakly.

"Kiri—" Eugeo started to say, then stopped.

Ring Vortex, overpowered by Mountain-Splitting Wave—he'd seen this exact sight before.

Yes, from this March, at the final match of the previous elite disciples' testing tournament. Volo's powerful sword had pushed Sortiliena down to one knee, just like Kirito was now...and then...

"Hraaahh!!"

Kirito roared again. The brilliant jade color flashed through his black sword once more, brightening the room. It was a combination of *two single-use attacks*. That was how Liena had defeated Volo in the end.

Normally, all secret techniques came to a halt if their form was broken. The only extension to their power came if the sword was pushed back along the same trajectory it initially followed. Liena saw it happen during Kirito and Volo's duel, then mastered it in just half a month—a dual use of the Serlut style's Ring Vortex.

Kirito had been Liena's page, but since she graduated right after the final testing match, he couldn't have had time to learn this right from her. He had made her technique his own, just from seeing it performed.

This was the proper way of a disciple and page.

This was the true nature of the sword.

Tears welled in Eugeo's left eye. They were tears of admiration for this incredible feat and tears of longing that he could have learned more in his short time. Through his blurred eye, he saw Kirito's second Ring Vortex snap Raios's sword in half...

And then it severed the first seat's hands, well above the wrist.

When Raios toppled onto the carpet, landing on his behind, he stared dumbfounded at his nearby broken sword half and the hilt piece, still clutched in his two loose hands. Eventually, his eyes traveled back to his own arms. They extended from his red sleeves, severed clean before the elbow. Jets of blood erupted from the sheer cross-sections, spilling more red on his chest and belly to match the color of his robe.

"A…aah…*aaaaaaaaahhh*!!" Raios screamed, his eyes bulging as far as they could go. "My…my arms!! My arrrrms!! The blood…the blood!!"

Just minutes ago, Raios had coldly told Humbert to stop whining and staunch the bleeding himself—apparently he was not made of sterner stuff himself. His eyes swiveled here and there until he at last spotted Humbert huddled a short distance away, and he tottered over on his knees.

"Humbeeeert!! Blood!! Stop my bleeding!! Take off your rope and tie my arms!!"

While Humbert typically acted like he was Raios's servant at these moments, he was unable to acquiesce in this instance. He cradled his own left arm, tied around several times with that special red rope, and shook his head in rapid motions. "N-no! If I t-take this off, my life will drop!!"

"What?! Humbert! You dare defy my orders…"

He stopped abruptly.

The two ropes used to tie up Tiese and Ronie were both tied around Humbert's stump. To stop the bleeding in Raios's arms, he'd need both. But without any treatment to stop his bleeding, removing the ropes from Humbert's arm would make the blood flow again, decreasing his life. And that—the intentional or unjustified lessening of another's life—was a grave breach of the Taboo Index.

"But…my blood…Humbert, you…Taboo…But…my life…" Raios babbled in a panicked falsetto. He looked back and forth frantically from his own gushing blood to the ropes tied around Humbert's wound.

As the heir to a third-rank noble family, Raios Antinous was placed in a hard spot, forced to choose between his own life and the Taboo Index. An amalgamation of his own swollen self-importance, he naturally valued his own life above anything else. But at the same time, he could not disobey the absolute authority of the Taboo Index. That would make him no better than Eugeo, whom he'd attempted to execute.

"Aaaah! Taboo...Life...Blood...Tabooooo...!" he wailed.

Kirito approached him, then stopped two mels short and reached out for Tiese and Ronie on the bed. He touched their shoulders to reassure them, nodded, then started to untie the rope that bound Ronie's top. Eugeo assumed he would use it to stop Raios's bleeding, but the knot was very tight. All the while, the first seat's howling and thrashing grew more frantic.

"Bluh...Tab...Lie...Ta...Live...Tab..." he grunted, back arched, barely forming words anymore. Kirito untied the rope at last and took a step toward the flailing man.

"Life, tagboo, live, daboo, dab, da, da, da-da-da-da—"

Raios's voice was turning abnormal. It sounded less human than animal, perhaps, or like the repetition of some broken tool.

"Da-da-da, dah, dah, dih, dil, dil-dil-dil, dildildildildi————"

The sound cut off.

Raios Antinous toppled straight backward. The blood was still flowing from his severed arms, meaning that he still had some essence of life left, but Eugeo sensed that Raios was no longer alive.

Likewise, Kirito, Tiese, and Ronie—who had been untying the other girl's ropes—were all frozen in shock. It was Humbert who first approached Raios to examine his strained rictus of a face.

"Aiiiie!" he screamed in terror. "R-R-Raios is...d-d-dead! K...k...killed...killed!! M-murder...Mo...mo...monster!!"

He crawled away from Kirito, then got to his feet, knees quaking, and rushed out into the common room. After that he exited to the hallway, as his footsteps and shrieks faded toward the stairs.

Eugeo had no idea what would happen next or what they should do. So many things had happened in such short succession that even his exploded eyeball seemed trivial. For now, he returned the Blue Rose Sword to its sheath and somehow managed to stand.

He met Kirito's eyes, nodded without a word, then plodded toward Tiese on the bed.

Then his feet stopped. Eugeo was a criminal now, guilty of cutting off Humbert's arm in violation of the Taboo Index. To that sixteen-year-old girl, he might be just as bad as Raios...perhaps even more detestable.

He slumped his head, unable to look up at her, and started to back away.

A small body slammed itself into his chest.

Red hair pressed hard against his uniform, and he heard an anguished voice cry, "I'm sorry...I'm sorry, Eugeo...I-It's all my fault—"

He shook his head, cutting off Tiese. "No, it's not your fault. I was...I didn't think it through. None of this is your fault."

"B-but...but..."

"It's okay. You and Ronie are safe, and that's what matters. I'm the one who should apologize...I'm sorry for putting you through this terror," he said, and patted the maple-red hair. Tiese began to bawl in earnest, and next to them, Ronie was weeping into Kirito's shirt in the same way. Eugeo's partner looked over her head at him and nodded.

Eugeo was going to nod back, but at that very moment, Kirito winced, as if someone had pulled on his hair. He looked left and right, then up at the ceiling.

When his eyes bulged, Eugeo followed their direction—and then he saw it.

On the ceiling of the bedroom, near the northeast corner, floated what looked like a purple board. It was similar to a Stacia Window but much larger, and round. On the inside, someone was watching the room...no, watching *them*. He couldn't tell if they were male or female, young or old. The skin was pale and white, and the eyes were like glass marbles.

...Where have I...?

......I've seen that face before. Long ago.

In that instant of recognition, the white face opened a mouth like a bottomless pit. Instantly, Kirito hissed into his ear, "Don't let the girls hear it!"

Eugeo promptly folded his arms around the sobbing Tiese's head. Kirito did the same to Ronie.

"*Singular Unit Detected. Tracing ID,*" spoke the person on the other side of the purple window in a bizarre voice. It sounded like sacred arts chanting, but he didn't recognize any of the vocabulary from class. After a few seconds, the face said, "*Coordinates Fixed. Report Complete.*"

And with that, the window vanished entirely. It was a freakish experience, but Eugeo's mind was too exhausted to feel shock or fear at this point. He exhaled and decided to leave the interpretation up to Kirito.

Outside the windows, the storm was receding, so the only sound in the room was Ronie's and Tiese's sobbing. Eugeo hugged his page tight and looked down at the floor.

There lay the corpse of Raios Antinous, frozen with his back in an extreme arch, thrusting his mangled arms outward. Kirito had cut off those arms, but Eugeo had done the same to Humbert, so they were both in the same boat. His mind replayed the sound of Humbert's voice:

Murderer. Monster.

Those words had appeared in his grandma's old stories, the ones she'd told Eugeo and his brothers to frighten them when they were little. The inhuman creatures in the land of darkness had no laws or taboos to keep, and they would murder even within their species, she said. Eugeo learned that fact for himself in that icy cave two years ago.

That's right...I'm just like those goblins now. I let my rage control me, and I struck down Humbert Zizek...a fellow student at my own school.

So shouldn't I at least judge and punish myself, to prove that I am not like those goblins in at least one tiny way? If I am a monster, do I really have the right to seek comfort in Tiese's warmth...?

He clenched his left eye shut and gritted his teeth—and that was when Kirito reached over and clamped his hand on Eugeo's shoulder.

"You're human, Eugeo. Just like me…You make mistakes, you try to find the meaning in them, and you keep struggling…like a human does."

The words prompted a sudden flood of warm liquid from Eugeo's left eye. He was afraid it had started bleeding like the one on the right, but when he carefully lifted the eyelid, he saw that the light of the lamp on the wall was glimmering and gleaming, broken into flickering pieces.

It wasn't blood he was looking through but tears. They fell down his cheek and landed in succession on Tiese's hair. After a few moments, she looked up at him. The hazy red of her eyes reminded him of leaves in the fall, laden with the droplets of morning dew.

His trainee page—at least for now—smiled the faintest of smiles, pulled a white cloth out of her pocket, and pressed it softly to his cheek. As the tears fell one after the other, Tiese silently continued to wipe them dry.

5

"…It is a terrible shame," murmured Miss Azurica, the dorm supervisor. She thought for a moment, then added, "I was certain that you two would be our school representatives at the end of the year."

"That was my plan, too," said Kirito, bold as ever. Unable to muster that same courage, Eugeo looked upward, feeling his left eye getting hot.

The May sky was utterly blue and cloudless, washed clean by the storm overnight. Birds crowded the green, budding branches, chirping brightly. It was the perfect day to lie down on the central lawn and take a nap—but they would never sleep at this school again.

Eugeo and Kirito had spent the night behind the heavy gate they had just left: the holding cells in the basement of the Swordcraft Academy faculty building. For hardly ever being used since the very founding of the school, the cell was quite thoroughly clean, and the bed was as nice as those at the primary trainee dorm, but Eugeo didn't get a wink of sleep.

Kirito, in characteristic form, worked hard through the night trying to heal Eugeo's ruptured eye with sacred arts, but without a catalyst, the best he could do was seal it up. Restoring its function was too difficult. He still didn't know why the eye had collapsed like that without an external cause. After a number of experiments, the spatial power dried up, and even Kirito's stubbornness had to be set aside.

At last the morning broke, and the sun shone through the narrow window. At the ringing of the nine o'clock bells, they were released at last. They figured that some imperial guardsmen had come to take them away, but to their surprise, it was merely Miss Azurica, the supervisor at the primary trainee dorm.

Kirito's statement caused the twentysomething teacher's expression to soften. Then she turned to Eugeo. Those silver-blue eyes, which put him in mind of polished metal, always made Eugeo nervous due to their resemblance to Sister Azalia's back home, but this time he stayed firm and met her gaze.

Azurica started to say something, then shut her mouth. Instead, she pulled an object out of her pocket—a pale-green sphere. It looked like a glass ornament, but it wasn't. It was a crystal of holy power, harvested from the school's Four Holy Flowers.

She squeezed the precious catalyst between her fingers and crushed it. The sphere shattered, the tiny pieces sparkling as they fell. She held out that hand to Eugeo's right eye and began to chant spell words.

"System Call. Generate Luminous Element..."

The chanting was far faster than any they'd heard from their sacred arts teacher. Eugeo and Kirito paused in shock as she smoothly assembled all the requisite words, until a warm light coalesced on Eugeo's wounded eye.

"Open your eye," she whispered. Very hesitantly, Eugeo lifted the eyelid that had been sealed for sixteen hours at this point. When he realized that his sight had returned in full capacity, he let out a gasp of surprise and delight. After several turns in place to assure himself that everything was truly normal, Eugeo came to his senses and bowed.

"Th-thank you, Miss Azurica."

"That's quite all right. More importantly, Disciple Eugeo and Disciple Kirito…I have something to say to you before you are handed over," Azurica announced. For a rare moment, she looked hesitant, then placed one hand each on their shoulders. "You are going to be judged for turning your backs on the Taboo Index and harming the life of others. But do not forget—the Taboo Index…the Axiom Church itself was created not by God but by man."

"Uh…wh-what does that…?" Eugeo started to ask.

Even small children knew that it was Stacia, god of creation, who forged the Earth. It was equally known that the Church that ruled the world was a holy creation as well.

"That is all I can say for now. But…I'm sure you will soon learn the truth of the world for yourselves," Azurica said. Then she winced and closed just her right eye. Eugeo could sense that she was feeling a sharp pain there.

"Disciple Eugeo…you broke a seal that I could not. That means you'll go places I could not reach…Trust in your sword and your friend," she said, then turned to the other boy. "Disciple Kirito. Here at the end, I still do not know just *who* you are. But I know that when you reach the tower, something will happen. I will be here, praying that you find the light."

Somehow, Kirito seemed to understand this mysterious statement. He nodded and enfolded Azurica's hand on his shoulder with both of his own, moving it to his chest. "Thank you, Miss Azurica. I'll come and see you again sometime. Then I can tell you everything you want to know."

Then he pulled her dainty fingers up to touch his lips. She blinked several times in surprise, and unless it was Eugeo's imagination, her cheeks seemed to color just a bit. She smiled faintly.

Kirito made that face like someone was tugging on his hair again, but she didn't seem to notice. She gently pulled her hand free of his, then removed the other one from Eugeo's shoulder.

"Let's go, then. Your escort is here."

*   *   *

The grounds of the school, usually bustling with students going to and from class, were eerily empty and quiet. Instead, Eugeo spotted something unexpected in front of the training hall. His freshly healed eyes bulged.

It was a huge creature, shining in the light of Solus. Not only was the metal armor on its chest and head gleaming, but so were the silvery-white triangular scales that covered its body. He didn't need to see the folded wings jutting up like twin towers or the long curved tail to know that it was a dragon. It was the largest and most powerful spiritual creature in the human empire, the mount of the Axiom Church's almighty Integrity Knights.

The dragon's rider was nowhere to be seen. Unperturbed by the massive dragon watching them from above, Miss Azurica walked the two boys to the entrance of the training hall and stopped.

She looked at both of them in turn, gave them a firm nod, then spun on her heels. As she strode away, tall boots clicking, both Kirito and Eugeo bowed deeply in her direction. Only when the footsteps were gone did they raise their heads, check on the dragon, and turn to the door.

"So…if there's a dragon…then does that mean our escort is… an Integrity Knight?" Eugeo whispered with a slight quiver. His partner snorted in his usual fashion and reached for the closed door.

"We'll find out soon," he said, pushed it open, and marched inside. Eugeo steeled his courage and followed.

It was gloomy inside, as the windows meant to bring in light were closed. Naturally, there were neither students nor instructors within the training floor and its stands.

On the wall across from the entrance, there was a painting based on the creation myth, that of the three goddesses of light vanquishing Vecta, god of darkness. But in the middle of the large, empty hall, facing toward the painting and away from them, there was a person.

Years ago, Eugeo had seen an Integrity Knight close up—when Alice was taken away. He'd called himself Deusolbert Synthesis

Seven and was nearly two mels tall. Whoever this was, they were far smaller. In fact, Eugeo was actually *taller*.

The blue cape that hung from the shoulder clasps was embroidered with the Axiom Church's insignia, a combination of cross and circle. But the most striking feature of the figure was the long, flowing golden hair. It reflected a deeper, richer glow than even Raios's, gleaming like molten gold in any level of light.

The Integrity Knight did not move, so Eugeo and Kirito shared a glance before starting forward. They crossed the training hall in a straight line, coming to a stop five mels before the short figure.

"...Elite Disciple Eugeo of the North Centoria Imperial Swordcraft Academy, at your service," he said awkwardly.

"Kirito, ditto."

Normally that would be when Eugeo would think, *Don't be lazy—introduce yourself properly!* but not even an inkling of that thought occurred to him now. And not due to nerves. As he gazed at the blue cape and golden hair, swaying gently in the breeze from the open door, a strange sensation started coming over him.

Where have I...?

The combination of blue and gold. It was...strangely...familiar...

Several seconds later, this constricting hesitation turned to full-blown, heart-stopping shock.

"Axiom Church of Centoria, Integrity Knight—Alice Synthesis Thirty."

The knight did not turn around for the introduction. But there was no way he would mistake that voice. He'd heard it nearly every day in the first ten years after his birth.

And the name. The last part was unfamiliar, but he couldn't miss the word *Alice*.

It couldn't be a coincidence. Eugeo stumbled forward, legs numb, and mumbled, "...Alice...? Is that you...? Are you... Alice...?"

Kirito reached out quickly from his side, but Eugeo slipped past his grasp to approach one step closer. The hair and cape rustled, sending forth a faint, light scent. It was gentle and familiar, like a field of flowers under the sun. It was the smell of his old friend's blue apron dress.

"Alice!" he called, firmly this time, and reached for her shoulder. She would turn around, greet Eugeo with that fond old smile, mischievous and smug—

A glint of light shattered that hope into dust.

A tremendous force smashed Eugeo's right cheek, knocking him clean off his feet to land heavily on the training hall floorboards.

"Eugeo!" Kirito cried, helping him up, but Eugeo was so stunned he didn't even register his friend's presence.

Somehow, there was a longsword in the knight's outstretched hand, even as she kept her back to them. But it was still sheathed, not naked. She had removed the sheath from its holder and used the end of it to strike Eugeo's cheek.

The knight smoothly lowered the sword and said, "Choose your words and actions carefully. I have the right to remove up to seventy percent of your life. The next time you attempt to touch me without permission, I will cut off your hand," she said, her voice as crisp, clear, and harsh as snowmelt water when she turned around at last.

"…Alice…"

Eugeo couldn't help mumbling that name one last time.

The Integrity Knight with the golden sword could be nobody else but the grown Alice Zuberg, daughter of Gasfut and sister of Selka, once taken away from Rulid as a child—Eugeo's childhood friend.

Naturally, she was not dressed the same. On her torso, shoulders, and waist was thin, light armor of finely detailed metal, and below that, the skirt extended practically to her ankles. But there was no mistaking that face.

Long, pristine blond hair. Clear, pale skin. But most of all, the incomparable deep blue of her slightly tapered eyes, a color that he'd never seen in anyone else's, even in Centoria.

But the look in those eyes was not what he remembered. The vibrant curiosity of her childhood Rulid days was gone, replaced by nothing but cold authority that fixed on Eugeo as he sat on the floor.

Her pink lips moved, producing that beautiful, cruel voice again. "Ahh...I intended to strike you for thirty percent of your life, but I achieved only half that. If you have the agility to disperse that damage, then I can see why you were able to achieve elite disciple status...and the boldness to attempt murder."

The way she spoke, it was as if she'd read Eugeo's Stacia Window without touching him, but he couldn't even begin to guess what that meant.

He just couldn't accept the words he was hearing. Kind, caring Alice would never say these things. Further, it made no sense that she had no reaction to his name, had struck him on the face without a second thought, and then—most of all—that she was standing there as an Integrity Knight, of all things.

He was going to call out again, to ignore her warning—when Kirito whispered into his ear.

"That knight must be the Alice you've been searching for."

Even in these bizarre circumstances, his partner's voice was calm and collected, and it brought a measure of rationality to Eugeo's bewildered mind. He managed to bob his head, to which Kirito whispered again, "Let's follow her orders for now. As long as we get into Central Cathedral, even as criminals, we should be able to argue our case."

Get into the cathedral.

It took Kirito's suggestion to get this point into Eugeo's head. His dream of going through the two tournaments in triumph and being named Integrity Knight was dead, but violating the Taboo Index had actually brought him here to his goal more than a year ahead of schedule.

Get into Central Cathedral and meet Alice. The order was backward now, but that was everything Eugeo wanted. He didn't know why she was acting like a totally different person now, but at the very least, he'd achieved half his goal. And once he got into the cathedral, he was sure to find a way to turn Alice back to her old self.

Eugeo's mind was back under rational self-control, and Alice was putting away her sword. She started walking for the main doors, cape trailing in the breeze.

"Stand and follow."

Disobedience was not an option. Kirito helped Eugeo up to his feet, and they followed her in silence.

Once out of the hall, Alice headed straight for the waiting dragon and patted its fearsome snout. Then she retrieved some strange tools from the large cargo bag behind the saddle. They looked like three heavy leather straps connected by chains—shackles. Just like the tool used to bind Alice eight years ago.

She brought over the shackles, one in each hand, then commanded Kirito and Eugeo to stand up straight. The order was far quieter than when Raios screamed that he would execute Eugeo, but it had a deep, irresistible quality to it, as though she were speaking God's own words.

"Elite Disciple Eugeo. Elite Disciple Kirito. You are hereby arrested for violating the Taboo Index and will be brought in for questioning and sentencing."

She wrapped the restraints around them as they stood at attention. The leather straps went around their arms, chest, and waist, and soon they were completely immobilized. She then returned to her dragon, still holding the chains connected to their backs, and fixed one chain to each of the large armor clasps on the beast's powerful haunches. Kirito was tied to the dragon's right leg and Eugeo to the left.

The Integrity Knight named Deusolbert had tied Alice to his dragon's leg the same way. But it was a day's flight from Rulid all the way to Centoria. If she was just dangling in thin air the entire time, it was hard to imagine a more terrifying, strenuous experience for an eleven-year-old.

Somehow, Alice was now an Integrity Knight herself, tying

Eugeo to her dragon just as she had once been tied. The lack of any hesitation in her actions forced Eugeo to face the truth: Alice the knight was both Alice Zuberg and a different person entirely. Some great and terrible power had changed her.

Like Kirito said, they might be able to learn the secret behind this change if they went to Central Cathedral. But the real question was, could they actually turn Alice back?

And even more pressing—what if the same thing happened to him? What if he forgot everything and turned into someone else? What if he forgot his life in Rulid, the journey to Centoria…even his memories at the academy…?

For a moment, he was plunged into deep fear and panic.

Then a pair of footsteps approached from behind, and both he and Kirito turned to look.

Stumbling forward, uncertain and yet insistent, was a pair of primary trainees in their gray uniforms: Tiese Schtrinen with her long red hair and Ronie Arabel with her brown hair cut short.

The hesitance of their footsteps was actually due to the objects they were carrying. Tiese had a longsword in a white leather sheath, while Ronie carried a similar weapon in black. It was clear at a glance that these were their personal swords, which had been left behind in Raios's bedroom.

Tiese's palms were split and bloodied where they held the sheath, and it was no wonder—even Eugeo and Kirito had to steel themselves to lift the swords, they were so heavy.

"Tiese…"

"Ronie!"

The girls responded with faint smiles through the pain. But it also drew the attention of Alice, who left the dragon's side to examine the girls. Eugeo recalled the stinging pain of the blow on his still-numb cheek, and he shouted, "No, Tiese! Don't come closer!"

But the trainees did not stop. They crossed the last ten mels of distance, blood dripping on the cobblestones, then fell to their knees in front of Alice.

After a lot of heavy breathing, Tiese was first to look up, face resolute, and said, "L-Lady Knight...we beg of you!"

Ronie followed in a quavering voice. "We ask your permission... to return their swords!"

Alice stared down at the girls until, eventually, she bobbed her head. "Very well. However, weapons cannot be given to the guilty. I will take them. If you wish to speak to them, you will have one minute."

She took the Blue Rose Sword in her right hand and the black sword in her left and easily lifted them up, apparently not feeling the weight whatsoever, then returned to the dragon and stashed the weapons in the storage bag from which she had pulled the restraints.

Tiese and Ronie clasped their bloodied hands before their chests, relief seeming to numb them to any pain. They unsteadily got to their feet and rushed to their tutors' sides.

"...Eugeo..."

Tiese leaned close, her red eyes puffy from crying. It took all of Eugeo's willpower to meet her gaze, rather than look away.

He had cut off Humbert's arm right in front of them last night. When the same fate befell Raios, he screeched in an unearthly manner before perishing. Tiese and Ronie were physically unharmed by the experience, but the mental shock and trauma had to be great.

To her, Eugeo was no longer a trustworthy mentor, but a criminal who had broken the Taboo Index. He was locked in chains, the only just fate for someone guilty of his sins.

But then—

Fat tears welled up in Tiese's maple-red eyes and spilled down her cheeks.

"Eugeo...I'm so sorry...This is...all my fault," she squeaked, clenching her hands. "I'm sorry...If only I hadn't...been so stupid..."

"No...that's not true," Eugeo said, stunned. "You did nothing wrong, Tiese…In fact, what you did for your friend was right. All of this…is my fault. You have nothing to apologize for."

She stared back into his eyes, so straightforwardly that she seemed to glimpse the very depths of his soul, and put on a brave smile.

"Next time," the young page said, quavering but resolute, "next time I will save *you*. I…I'll work my hardest, become an Integrity Knight, and come save you…so just be patient. Wait for me. I swear…I swear…"

A sob stuck the words in her throat. Eugeo could do nothing but nod.

On the other side of the dragon, Ronie and Kirito finished a similarly short conversation. She put a small package into Kirito's chained hands and tearfully said, "This is…a lunch for you. If you get hungry, please eat…"

Whatever Kirito said in reply was drowned out by the sound of the dragon's wings flapping.

"It is time. Step away," Alice commanded from the saddle. She whipped the reins, and the dragon stood. The chains pulled upward and left Eugeo nearly in the air.

Tiese and Ronie took a few steps backward, tears tumbling from their eyes. The silver wings beat the air, whipping the girls' hair around.

The dragon took a few rumbling steps to pick up speed. The girls sprinted after them, but soon they stumbled and dropped to all fours. Then the beast's powerful legs launched off the surface and into the air.

As it ascended in a spiral, Tiese and Ronie grew smaller and smaller. Eventually they disappeared into the gray blur of the cobblestones, and even the entirety of the North Centoria Imperial Swordcraft Academy began to fade.

The dragon, Integrity Knight on its back and criminals hanging from its legs, started a direct flight to the Axiom Church's towering Central Cathedral at the heart of everything.

INTERLUDE III

In the middle of the massive *Ocean Turtle* marine research facility was a vertical shaft sixty feet across and over three hundred feet deep.

This Main Shaft, which was reinforced with titanium alloy, both supported the ship's various floors and protected its central functions. In addition to the ship's control and propulsion systems, it housed the mysterious Rath's many advanced machines.

There were four Soul Translators (STLs)—incredible full-dive machines capable of reading and writing the human soul—and, connected to them, one Lightcube Cluster that served as their mainframe.

The cluster was installed right in the center of the shaft. STL Units Two and Three were in the Lower Shaft, while Units Four and Five were in the Upper Shaft. STL prototype Unit One wasn't on the ship but in Rath's Roppongi office far away.

Kirito—Kazuto Kirigaya—was currently in Unit Four, connected to the system as a means of repairing his neural network while he struggled to recover from his coma. So in order to reach him, they had to enter the shaft at the bottom and take an elevator to the upper portion.

It was 7:30 AM on Monday, July 6th, 2026.

Asuna Yuuki adjusted the collar of the loose summer sweater she wore over her T-shirt as she climbed the dim spiral staircase.

Her feet sounded loudly on the galvanized metal steps, lit by the orange emergency LED lights. The experience couldn't help but remind her of a place far, far from here, in a metal castle floating in an infinite sky, where she climbed many staircases like this one—those spiral stairs that connected the boss chamber of each floor of Aincrad with the next one above…

In most cases, she had walked behind Heathcliff, leader of the Knights of the Blood, with the other guild members celebrating their triumph behind them, but there were exceptions. Before she joined the KoB, near the very start of the game of death, she walked with a solo player dressed all in black.

With his easy, aloof manner that belied the exhaustion of battle, he would tell bad jokes to annoy her or give her information on the next floor. On those few occasions, he was the one to guide her onward when she felt crushed by the fatigue of their endless quest.

"…Kirito…"

She mumbled the name of her lover under the sound of her clanking footsteps.

There was no answer, of course.

She pushed down the welling sensation of loneliness that threatened to overcome her. Unlike just two days ago, Kazuto was no longer missing. He was waiting for her in that little room at the top of these stairs. She couldn't converse with him yet—but even if she couldn't hold his hand, she knew his awakening was approaching, moment by moment. Natsuki Aki, his nurse, said that if the STL's treatment continued well, his neural network might be repaired within a day or two, moving him toward the stage of consciousness again.

Asuna hadn't explained everything to her parents about the journey to the *Ocean Turtle* floating off the Izu Islands. She'd enlisted the help of Dr. Rinko Koujiro to explain to them that she would be assisting the doctor on an observation of a high-tech research facility for the next few days—an explanation that wasn't *entirely* untrue.

She knew it was a weak excuse, but her mother, Kyouko Yuuki, just gave Asuna a searching look, then said, "Take care." Perhaps she instinctually understood everything that was going on.

At any rate, Asuna had only three days of time here, from July 5th to the 7th. That meant that tomorrow evening, she had to be on the regularly scheduled helicopter going from the *Ocean Turtle* to the heliport back in Shinkiba. She didn't know if she'd be making that return trip to Tokyo with Kazuto yet, but if Nurse Aki was right, she'd at least be able to talk to him.

When that happened, she'd get her chance to rage at him, to cry, and to laugh.

She stopped in the middle of the staircase, took a deep breath, then resumed climbing.

After another twenty steps, the stairs came to an abrupt end. It wasn't a dead end; there was a heavy round hatch in the ceiling, through which she needed to climb a retracting ladder.

That layer of metal, eight inches thick, was the titanium composite wall that split the upper and lower halves of the Main Shaft. Lieutenant Nakanishi bragged that it was strong enough to protect against rifle fire at close range, but it was unclear why such a situation would arise on a nonmilitary mega-float.

Between him and Mr. Kikuoka, these people sure like to make grandiose statements, Asuna thought as she ascended the aluminum alloy ladder through the hatch. The dark spiral staircase continued after that, but the lights were green up above. It really was as if she'd ascended to a new floor in a game.

Now she was in the Upper Shaft, where they kept the Lightcube Cluster, the physical center of the entire Alicization Project. It was probably just on the other side of the staircase wall, in fact.

The Lightcube Cluster was top secret, so she didn't really know how it worked other than that it was a literal cluster of an extreme number of lightcubes, as the name stated.

Lightcubes were the physical media that stored the artificial fluctlights—the "souls" of the Underworldians who functioned as bottom-up AIs—and they had lined up hundreds of thousands of them around one enormous cube. Instead of souls, that cube contained the massive amount of mnemonic visual data for all the Underworldians. It was the core of the STL, the Main Visualizer...

Takeru Higa, Rath's chief researcher, had explained the Underworld's workings to Asuna in a general sense, skipping over some company secrets here and there, but to be honest, it still sounded like a bunch of gibberish to her.

When she suggested they let her see the Lightcube Cluster itself, given all the things they were telling her, Higa seemed a bit flustered and said the cluster's metal shell just made it look like a big box. And nobody could open it now—not Higa, not the other staff members, not even project overseer and SDF Lieutenant Colonel Seijirou Kikuoka.

So all Asuna could do was imagine a vague concept of the cluster. Endless rows of tiny crystals, lined up in darkness. Between the perfect square of their array and the larger crystal in the center, fine little lines of light were threading to and fro, like the stars clustered at the center of a galaxy...

She was so lost in thought envisioning the image that Asuna was slow to notice someone coming down the stairs from above.

"Oh, sorry," she said automatically, dodging to the left. The other person continued by without a word. With each descending stair, the footstep made a *zshunk, vweem* sound.

"Hmn...?"

A part of her brain latched on to that strange sound, and just as the figure passed her position, she looked up and stared to the right.

"Ah...?!"

Instantly, she backed away, pressing herself against the wall.

The question wasn't *who* was coming down the stairs but *what*. Because whatever it was, it was not a human being.

The overall silhouette was humanoid, but instead of a skeleton, it had a bare metal frame with resin-cased cylinders attached to its limbs and waist. Fine exposed gears made up its joints, and colored signal cables ran up and down its length like arteries.

On its back was a large box, while its "face" was just three lenses: large, medium, and small. Asuna subconsciously wondered why they hadn't just put two identically sized lenses for eyes, then realized what she was thinking.

She let out the breath she was holding and whispered, "A... robot...?"

Instantly, the mysterious bipedal machine stopped moving. The gears in its legs whirred, pulling back the foot to its previous perch. Once it was standing on the same step as Asuna, it rotated its body in place to the left to face her. The two bigger lenses were dark, but there was a red light in the small one, flickering unevenly as though watching her.

"Mm—!"

A little squeak escaped from her throat. She tried to back away, but she was already pressed against the wall of the stairwell. Asuna leaned right, then left, but the red light continued tracking her face.

Monsters aren't supposed to pop up on the staircases between floors—and there're no robot mobs in the first place—and anyway, I'm in real life, not a game! Her mind raced from thought to thought, and she was about to turn and dart back down the way she had come when there was a voice from above.

"Hey! Knock it off, Ichiemon!"

A man was descending the stairs with an expression of alarm. He wore a print T-shirt, shorts, thick metal-framed glasses, and had his short hair spiked back—this was the lead researcher on Project Alicization, Takeru Higa himself. He had a well-used laptop in his hand.

The machine-man pulled its lenses away from Asuna and rotated ninety degrees toward Higa, as though reacting to his spoken command.

Asuna finally relaxed, then looked at the researcher on the next step upward and demanded, "Mr. Higa...what is this?"

"Er, well…it's Ichiemon. The official name is Electroactive Muscled Operative Machine, or EMOM, and it's the first of its type, so 1EMOM—which we've nicknamed Ichiemon," he answered, his expression shifting between embarrassment and pride.

She glared at him and asked, "And…what is Ichiemon doing here?"

It wasn't Higa who answered the question. "Higa's just helping me fine-tune my program. I don't know why—it's not like we're cohorts back at the college seminar anymore."

That answer came from a woman descending the stairs behind him. She had a white lab coat over her denim shirt and jeans, and her hair was parted straight down the side, a look that screamed *intellectual*. This was Dr. Rinko Koujiro, the very person who helped Asuna infiltrate the *Ocean Turtle*.

"Good morning, Asuna."

"Good morning," she replied, then gave Ichiemon another examination from top to bottom and asked the researchers, "This…isn't part of Project Alicization, too, is it?"

Ichiemon took the lead back up the spiral staircase until they reached the sub-control room, where Asuna finally pushed her questions aside and rushed down the hallway to the STL room.

She couldn't go in the door at the end of the narrow tunnel, but the left-hand wall was made of clear reinforced glass. She pressed her hands and forehead against the window and peered into the barely lit storage room.

The two massive rectangular objects were Soul Translator Unit Four and Unit Five. Unit Five was powered down, but there were a number of soft lights, some of them blinking, active on Unit Four. If she squinted, she could see a thin silhouette on the gel bed connected to the main device.

That was Kirito, aka Kazuto Kirigaya. Asuna's partner in so many different ways.

A week ago, a suspect in the Death Gun incident had attacked

Kazuto on the street in Setagaya Ward. The attacker injected him with deadly succinylcholine, temporarily paralyzing his heart.

Emergency measures were successful at preventing his death, but the stoppage of blood flow had damaged his brain—the doctor said that Kazuto might even be in a permanent vegetative state. In the end, it was Lieutenant Colonel Seijirou Kikuoka, leader of the Alicization Project, who flew him here to the *Ocean Turtle* on life support. He claimed that it was a difficult decision that he'd made with the belief that the STL could help heal Kazuto.

Apparently, Kazuto's mind was currently in a medical-use VR environment called the Underworld. By activating his consciousness—his fluctlight—they hoped to regenerate his neural network. It was hard to understand everything they were trying to explain to her, but she at least understood that he wasn't in a simple coma now.

She was looking at only his body; his mind was in a far-off virtual world. She supposed this was how Kazuto had felt while Nobuyuki Sugou held her captive in the fairy world of Alfheim.

If only I could do what he did back then and go dive into the Underworld to save him...

After over a minute of watching and thinking, Asuna pulled away from the glass. She gave him a silent promise to return by midday, then returned to Subcon.

Compared to the main control room in the Lower Shaft, this room was quite small. The control console was a simplified version, too, and the desks and chairs here were cheap.

Higa and Rinko stood at the desk rather than using the chairs. They set up the laptop on the desk, accompanied by the frightening Ichiemon.

Once she was certain the robot was on standby and wouldn't make any sudden moves, Asuna approached the two adults. In college, they'd been members of the same seminar—along with Akihiko Kayaba and Nobuyuki Sugou, in fact—and they were debating the project in the rapid-fire informal conversation of old friends.

"I think the bottleneck's in the balancer's processing. Don't you have the budget for faster chips?"

"We're at maximum capacity if you consider cooling and battery usage. Our only option is to pick up slack by tuning the EAP actuators…"

"But those polymer muscles are so last-generation. Use CNT and it'll lighten right up."

"N-now, *that's* a surefire way to kill our budget…but we do have enough for one unit, I suppose…"

"Still haven't gotten over your need to skimp on materials, huh?" Rinko said, shaking her head. She noticed Asuna standing there and ducked her head guiltily. "Oh, I'm so sorry, Asuna. I didn't mean to be so noisy."

"Actually, I think Kirito likes it when things are lively," she replied with a grin, then looked at the robot. From what she could understand of their conversation, the actuators moving its body were artificial muscles made of organic materials. It was cutting-edge technology, for sure, but seemed unrelated to Rath's main work in developing AI.

Higa seemed to sense her skepticism. He leaned back against the table and said, "The old guy wanted us to make this, too."

"Uh…Mr. Kikuoka does? But why…?"

"Well, I'm not sure how serious he is about it." Rinko sighed. "But if we're going to bring the fluctlights from the Underworld back here, they'll need a body to move around in, right?"

"Then…then this robot is meant to house an AI?"

"That seems to be the plan."

"Yep, exactly."

Rinko and Higa answered the last one together. Asuna gave Ichiemon another piercing examination. The overall form was human, yes, but the frame was too blocky, the joints jutting out, and no amount of silicone rubber was going to hide that and make it look like a person.

"…No disrespect to Ichiemon, but…won't the AIs be shocked if they have to live in a body like this…?"

At the very least, Asuna and Kazuto's top-down AI "daughter," Yui, would absolutely refuse to inhabit such a thing, she suspected.

Higa waved frantically. "Oh, no, no, we wouldn't put them in this. Ichiemon's just a prototype for data collection. His processor's using old architecture, which is why he's so chunky. We have a second unit for testing with onboard AI, and that one's much more advanced."

"Second unit…And would that one's name be…?"

"Niemon," he answered matter-of-factly.

"Ah…for 'two.' I should have figured," she said, shaking her head. "So what is it that makes the onboard-AI prototype more advanced?"

"Well, its sensors and balancers are way, way more effective at their job…or so we hope," Rinko answered for Higa. She stepped sideways and, for some reason, pulled her feet together and balanced on tiptoe. Then she spread her arms a bit and held that position, wavering slightly.

"Even when we human beings are standing still, our entire bodies are working to fine-tune our balance—almost entirely unconsciously, in fact. Even right now, as I'm struggling not to fall over, I'm not thinking, 'I'm leaning this far to the right, so I need to straighten my right leg more than my left.' My brain—my fluctlight—is controlling my muscles and bones with its own autobalancing function."

She dropped her sneaker heels back to the floor and grinned. "Ichiemon has servos that re-create that autobalancing function through mechanical and electronic means. But like you saw when he was slowly going up and down the stairs, it takes a huge number of sensors and balancers, a high-powered CPU, batteries, and cooling systems, plus a frame strong enough to support all those things. That's why we can't make Ichiemon any smarter than he already is."

"Even this is way more human than we could get a decade ago." Higa smirked.

"Meaning...if its brain functions aren't handled by an old CPU but an artificial fluctlight, it should have the same balancing ability that any human being does?" Asuna asked.

"Yep! That's the idea. That way we can shrink the servos to a fraction of the size, make the frame lighter, the actuators smaller, and get it far closer to the actual human body...we hope. It's still a bit of a pipe dream. Like I said, Niemon is much more human—well, the silhouette is, anyway."

"Well, if you're that proud of it, show us alr—" Rinko started to say, then stopped herself. She frowned, deep in thought, then said in a much lower voice, "Higa...Niemon can't walk around autonomously yet, can it?"

"Huh? Of course not. It's got the CPU in there, but the actual control program's just an empty shell. Even if you loaded Ichiemon's program, the difference with Niemon's sensory systems would make it fall over by the third step, I bet."

"...Oh..."

Rinko considered this, then took a deep breath and turned to Asuna to change the topic. "Have you had breakfast yet?"

"Not yet."

"Then let's go to the mess hall. Higa's going to eat here with Ichiemon."

Asuna thought that was a joke, but Higa pulled an energy bar out of his shorts pocket and waved them off with a "Take your time." Asuna shook her head in equal parts exasperation and wonder, then followed Rinko.

Before she left, she looked at the STL room and mouthed the words *I'll be back.*

In the hallway leading away from Subcon, someone was approaching from the elevator. It was two men, in fact, both wearing lab coats over T-shirts. They were probably more of Rath's employees, of which there were supposedly at least a dozen, but Asuna didn't know their names yet. They probably still assumed that she was Rinko's assistant, the way she had been disguised when she'd snuck aboard.

She bowed to them after Rinko, and as the two men passed, she followed them out of the corner of her eye. She didn't recognize the profile of the man with the scruffy whiskers and the ponytail. But something itched in the back of her mind. It was that sense of danger that, if back in Aincrad, would at least have her hand on the hilt of her rapier, if not drawing it entirely...

"What is it, Asuna?" Rinko asked quietly, and she realized that she had stopped still. The men continued down the hall, flip-flops slapping against the floor as they made their way to Subcon.

"...No. It's nothing."

They continued walking, Asuna attempting to pin down the source of that strange sensation all the while. But after she exhausted the possibilities, it began to fade away and eventually vanished.

CHAPTER SIX

PRISONERS AND KNIGHTS, MAY 380 HE

1

Even now, there were times I thought back to when I was held prisoner in Aincrad.

Back then, especially that first year of the game of death, every single day lasted forever. Whenever I was outside of town, I had to watch my back at all times for monster (and occasionally player) attacks, and leveling at maximum efficiency required some truly grueling daily schedules.

I cut down my sleeping time as far as I could without sacrificing concentration, and I dedicated even the scant time I had for eating to memorizing data I bought from info brokers. By the later stages of the game, I was the black sheep of the advancement group, a guy who could spend an entire day taking a nap, but I never thought of myself as simply wasting my time. It felt like the fourteen years before *SAO* and the two years in Aincrad occupied an equal amount of time in my mind.

Compare that to this...

The days since coming to this mysterious Underworld seemed to fly by. I wasn't letting them slip past out of laziness—not at all. If anything, the two years from leaving Rulid to joining the Zakkaria garrison to being a student at the Swordcraft Academy in Centoria were a time of constant activity. Perhaps even busier than my time in *SAO*. And yet when I thought back on them, it felt as though they'd passed in a blink.

Perhaps the reason for that was the lack of danger of my life—their concept of HP—running down to zero. Or perhaps the reason was that compared to real life, the passage of time here was vastly accelerated.

When I took on a job for the mysterious tech company Rath, they explained that the maximum FLA (fluctlight acceleration) of the STL was three times that of normal time. But that was probably—no, definitely—false. Based on a number of data, I estimated that my current FLA ratio was closer to a thousand to one. If true, then the two years I'd spent in this simulation had passed in just eighteen hours in the real world. Surely the lack of mortal danger and the knowledge that all of this was passing in the blink of a (real-world) eye were making the days feel shorter.

But...no.

Perhaps there was another reason.

It was because my life here...especially at the Swordcraft Academy, with Eugeo, Sortiliena, Ronie, and Tiese, had been so enjoyable. Even though what brought me to the school to polish my skills was to get *out* of this place as soon as possible. Perhaps my secret desire for this enjoyment to last was making the time pass quicker.

If so, that was a betrayal. A betrayal of Asuna, Sugu, Sinon, and the others, all waiting and worrying about me in the real world.

Perhaps this was my punishment for that betrayal. My time at the academy ended in a bloody catastrophe and got me locked down beneath the earth, where no ray of sunshine could penetrate...

I stopped reflecting and sat up, causing the steel chain locked around my right wrist to clink. A few moments later, I heard a dull whisper from the darkness nearby.

"...You awake, Kirito?"

"Yeah...have been for a while. Sorry, did that wake you?" I

whispered back, so as not to attract the attention of the jailer. I heard a dry, exhaled chuckle.

"Of course I can't sleep. I'm normal—not like someone else who started snoring away from the moment we got locked in here."

"That's the second secret to the Aincrad style: Sleep when you get the chance," I improvised, then glanced around us.

We were surrounded by deep darkness, with the only light coming from the jailer's station down the hall on the other side of the steel bars. If I squinted, I could just make out the silhouette of Eugeo on the adjacent bed.

I'd mastered the elementary-level sacred art of sparking a light on the end of a stick long ago, of course, but this prison was thorough enough to block any kind of spellcasting inside it.

I looked in the direction of Eugeo's face, though I couldn't make out his expression, and, after mulling it over, asked, "Well…feeling a bit calmer now?"

My internal clock told me it was about three in the morning. If we were locked in this basement prison at midday yesterday, that meant only thirty-five hours or so had passed since the incident of two nights before. Eugeo defied the Taboo Index to attack Humbert Zizek with his Blue Rose Sword, then witnessed Raios Antinous lose his mind and die—an almost incalculable amount of shock and trauma for him to undergo.

After a long silence, an even softer voice responded, "It feels like…all this has been a dream…That I turned my sword on Humbert…and that Raios ended up like *that*…"

"…Don't think too hard about it. You need to focus on what comes after this instead."

It was the best I could come up with. I wished I could rub his back to reassure him, but the chains kept me from reaching the other bed. After a few moments of watching his outline closely, I heard him whimper, "Got it. I'll be all right."

I was the one who had severed Raios Antinous's wrists, not Eugeo. The wounds themselves shouldn't have been fatal if treated promptly and properly, but I suspected that he got stuck in an infinite mental loop trying to assign priority between his own life and the Taboo Index, which caused his fluctlight to collapse.

I did feel guilt at causing the death of an Underworldian, of course. But already, two years ago, I'd killed two goblins in the cave north of Rulid to save Selka, the sister in training. They had fluctlights just like Raios did, so it would almost be an insult to that goblin captain's memory if I fell to pieces over killing Raios, who was far weaker than them.

But even then, something sat wrong with me.

My running suspicion was that Rath and Seijirou Kikuoka, the people operating the Underworld, were attempting to create a true artificial intelligence.

The artificial fluctlights here already had emotions and intelligence on par with real human beings. If their one flaw was absolute, blind obedience to the law, then Eugeo had crossed that wall by drawing his Blue Rose Sword and striking Humbert down to save Tiese and Ronie. In other words, he'd completed his final breakthrough and evolved into true artificial intelligence.

And yet, thirty-five hours of internal time later, the world showed no signs of shutting down. Either the acceleration rate was so high that Rath still hadn't noticed the change or there was some kind of horrible accident going on that I couldn't even imagine…

"What comes…after this," Eugeo repeated from the other bed. I set aside my concerns and took my eyes off the ceiling to look at him again. In the darkness, his familiar silhouette bobbed and continued, "You're right, Kirito. We've got to get out of this prison and find out what happened to Alice…"

I was relieved that my partner seemed to be recovering from his shock, but something very important in his statement stuck with me. He'd said, "Get out of this prison" like it was just that simple. To him, this prison—a symbol of the Axiom Church's power if there ever was one, the place we would remain until we received God's forgiveness—was less important than Alice. The recent events had indeed prompted a major change in the way his mind worked.

But I didn't have time to delve into that now. Soon the sun would rise, and some inquisitor or executioner would come drag us out. Like Eugeo said, we could consider deeper matters once we had escaped.

"Yeah...I'm sure there must be a way to get out."

But only if it's your typical RPG locked-in-a-jail event, where there's always a means of escape.

I brushed the chains holding me in place. They were cold and almost unbearably tough metal. They were welded to a ring of the same material that was locked around my wrist, which in turn was connected to a similar ring embedded in the wall. It was quite clear that no amount of pulling would break any part of the binding apparatus.

Yesterday morning, Eugeo and I had finally crossed the wall into the Axiom Church's Central Cathedral, our ultimate goal ever since leaving the very northern tip of the world. We hadn't planned on doing it by dangling from the legs of a dragon, however.

We had barely had any time to admire the chalk-white tower that stretched up into the clouds before they sent us marching down a deep spiral staircase behind the spire, and at last we reached this underground prison and were handed over to its fearsome jailer.

Alice Synthesis Thirty had finished her duty and left without a word. After that, the beastly, burly jailer with a metal mask like a kettle slowly but surely chained us here in this cell.

For food that night, we got one meal of hard, dried bread and a skin of lukewarm water, tossed through the bars. Compared to this, even the treatment of the orange players in the jail at Black-iron Palace in Aincrad was like a suite at a luxury hotel.

We'd tried and failed at every method of freedom yesterday: pulling on the chains, gnawing, sacred arts. If we had the Blue

Rose Sword or my black one, we could cut through them like butter, but sadly, the weapons that the girls tore their palms bloody to bring to us had been taken who-knew-where by Alice. Ronie's homemade lunch thankfully escaped confiscation, but it was now long gone.

In short, we just "needed a way out." However, we'd tried and failed at every conceivable option so far.

"I wonder...if Alice was chained up down here, too..." Eugeo mumbled, sitting on the bed of metal frame and rags.

"Yeah...dunno," I said, which was not much of an answer. If Alice Zuberg, Eugeo's childhood friend and Selka's sister, had undergone the same treatment, that meant she'd been locked in this horrible place alone by that iron-masked jailer at the tender age of eleven. It was hard to imagine a more terrifying experience.

Eventually she would have been summoned to make a confession, then sentenced—and then what...?

"Say, Eugeo. Stop me if I'm off, but...are you absolutely certain that this Alice Synthesis Thirty is the same person as the Alice you're looking for?" I asked hesitantly.

After a few seconds, a pained response came: "That voice...her golden hair and blue eyes...I'd never forget them. That was Alice. But...otherwise, she seemed like a totally different person..."

"For being old friends, she sure smashed you pretty good. So perhaps...her memories are being controlled in some fashion... or her thoughts limited, even...?"

"But there were no sacred arts like that listed in the textbook."

"But the fancy bishops of the Church can manipulate life itself, right? Surely they've got some means to mess around with memories."

And in fact, the Soul Translator I was using to dive into the Underworld could do just such a thing. If they could manipulate the memory of a biological brain, surely it would be even easier and more effective on an artificial fluctlight saved on its own medium.

"But," I continued, "if that knight is the real Alice, then what was that *thing* two years ago, in the cave north of Rulid…?"

"Right…you mentioned that, when you were healing me with Selka, you heard a voice that sounded like Alice's…"

Though I hadn't told Eugeo all the details, I'd used Selka's powers to give him half my life when he was gravely wounded in the fight with the goblins. It was a very risky action and sucked out my life at a much faster pace than I'd expected, but just when I was certain that I couldn't maintain myself any longer—I had heard a voice.

"Kirito, Eugeo…I'll be waiting for you always…I am waiting for you at the top of Central Cathedral…"

Along with the voice, I had felt a mysterious warm light fill me, restoring both my life and Eugeo's. That wasn't just confused memory. It must have been Alice, once taken away by the Axiom Church, using some unexplained power to save us.

We took that message to heart and had made our way down to Centoria to the Central Cathedral.

But when we finally met Alice in a most unexpected manner, she was not Alice Zuberg from Rulid but the Integrity Knight Alice Synthesis Thirty. She treated us merely as criminals to be judged and gave no sign whatsoever that she was Eugeo's childhood friend.

Either she was a different person who coincidentally shared her looks and name or she was the real Alice with her memories altered or controlled. It seemed the only way we'd find out the truth was to escape this prison and actually get up to the top of Central Cathedral—the place where we'd find out everything about the Axiom Church.

And yet we hadn't been able to put a scratch on the chains or bars so far and didn't seem likely to in the future.

"Argh, this is so frustrating…If there's a God here, I'd like to strangle that holy neck until I finally get the entire truth!" I grunted, thinking of Seijirou Kikuoka's stupid face.

Eugeo chuckled nervously and whispered, "Come on, you shouldn't insult Stacia while we're inside the church. You don't want divine retribution."

His shift in priorities regarding the Taboo Index had not removed his faith in their religion, I noted, and added, "Hey, maybe she'll punish these chains instead."

Then a thought occurred to me, and I changed my tone. "Wait a second. Speaking of Stacia, couldn't we call up a window here?"

"You know, we never thought to try that. Go on and see."

"Right."

I waited to ensure that there wasn't any movement from the jailer's station down the hallway to the left, then extended the index and middle finger of my right hand. I made the familiar status window summoning gesture, then tapped the chain tied to my left hand.

After a brief pause, a pale-purple window popped into being. I didn't think that learning the chain's properties was going to improve our situation, but it never hurt to have more information.

"Hey, there it is!" Eugeo grinned and checked the numbers. There were just three lines of information: the object ID, a horrifying *23,500/23,500* durability rating, and the descriptor *class-38 object*. Class 38 was a higher value than many fine swords, but it was lower than the Blue Rose Sword's 45 and the 46 for the black sword made from the Gigas Cedar branch. If we had either sword, we could cut through the chains—but it was pointless to hope for that now.

Eugeo popped up the window on his own chains and groaned. "Ugh, no wonder they wouldn't budge even the tiniest bit. We'll need at least a class-38 weapon or tool to cut them…"

"That's exactly right," I said, looking around the dim cell, but all the room contained was the crude metal beds and an empty waterskin. I felt a brief moment of hope when I wondered if I could remove a leg of my bed to use as a crowbar, but upon examining the window, it was a cheap class-3 object. The iron bars looked much tougher, but the chain was too short for me to reach them.

I looked around, even more desperate for some option I hadn't tried yet, when Eugeo said weakly, "You're not going to suddenly find some incredible sword hiding in your cell. I mean, what's there to find? It's just the beds, the skin, and these chains."

"Just…chains…" I mumbled, staring at the chain confining my arm, then the one around Eugeo's wrist. Suddenly, I had an idea. I tried to control my excitement. "It's not *just* chains. It's two damn chains!"

"Huhhh?" Eugeo gasped, totally baffled. I waved him down off the bed, then got onto the stone floor myself so I could see my partner's outline standing in the darkness, wearing the school uniform he'd had on since our arrest.

Around his right wrist was a crude metal ring, like mine, welded to a long chain that ran to a fastener in the wall behind his bed.

First, I ducked under Eugeo's chain, then doubled back over it to my original spot. That crossed our chains into an X pattern. Then I motioned for him to back away, which I did as well, so that the tension at the intersection of the chains was high enough for them to creak unpleasantly.

At last, Eugeo seemed to understand what I was thinking. "Um, Kirito, you aren't suggesting that we both pull, are you?"

"Pull, indeed. The two chains have identical priority levels, so this should essentially damage the life of both. We'll see once we try—use both hands to pull."

Eugeo still seemed skeptical, but he did as I said and used both hands to grab the chain connected to his right wrist, then crouched a bit. I did the same on my end.

"Wait, before that…"

I made the sigil with my left hand and called up the chain's window again.

If we tried this method in the real world in an attempt to sever chains of this thickness, we'd maybe put a tiny scratch on the surface at best. But in the Underworld, no matter how real every-thing looked, the physical principles were different. As dem-onstrated by the way we cut through a twelve-foot-wide tree in just a few days with the divine Blue Rose Sword, when any two objects collided with a certain amount of force and velocity, the higher-priority object would eventually destroy the other.

We made eye contact to get our timing right, then yanked on the chains with all our might.

Gink! The chains rattled, dull and forceful, and it took my entire core to keep my legs planted so that Eugeo's surprising brute strength didn't hurtle me off my feet. He started to get into the spirit of it, too, and before long we had mostly forgotten the original idea and were having a simple tug-of-war.

In addition to the ugly scraping at the intersection of the chains, there were occasional orange flashes of sparks. Without letting up any of the pressure, I craned my neck to check the open status window.

"Oh!"

I couldn't pump my fist with both hands occupied, so I had to smirk instead. The durability value was descending, with the ones digit rotating faster than I could see and the tens digit dropping fast. At this rate, we'd have them down to zero in mere minutes. I gritted my teeth, pulling even harder with Eugeo.

In order for this to work, we had to have two chains and two pris-oners, as well as a high-enough object control authority—what would correspond to the strength stat in *SAO*—to override the chains' level. So it was unlikely that eleven-year-old Alice, imprisoned alone, would have been able to do this.

She must have gone to her interrogation, and then something happened. If the two Alices were the same person, then they must have done something to her that controlled her mind, changing her into an obedient soldier of the Axiom Church...

I was so occupied by this train of thought that I forgot a very crucial part of the plan. We needed to stop tugging just before the life of the chains went down to zero. Otherwise...

Ping! That sound was much higher-pitched than the previous. The next instant, Eugeo and I were hurtling backward, and I slammed the back of my head against the hard stone wall.

I huddled on the ground, clutching my head, desperately trying to resist the pain and dizziness the STL faithfully represented. Once they abated, I looked toward the door, certain that the jailer would have heard us this time, but there was no reaction. I exhaled with relief and got up.

When Eugeo recovered and stood on his own, he rubbed his head and muttered, "Ow…that must have knocked a hundred off my life."

"Hey, that's a cheap price to pay. Check it out."

I held out my right arm, the chain dangling limp from the shackle. The metal was severed clean, with about one mel and twenty cens left connected. There were four U-shaped pieces of metal on the ground, the remains of the two rings that had split simultaneously from the stress of our pulling. Before long, they tinkled and crumbled out of existence.

That gave me the idea to check the window of the broken chain hanging from my arm. It had recovered its life up to 18,000, nearly the original amount. My expectation (more like hope) was that once we pulled its life down to zero, the entire three-mel length of the chain would be obliterated as a whole, but because it was made of a long series of rings, the remaining parts had instead reconstituted as new chain objects.

Eugeo checked his own chain, following the same line of thought, then threw up his shoulders and said, "Good grief…I could never pull off a mad idea like this. It's why I'll never be like you, Kirito."

"Heh! My motto is, 'Impossible, improbable, inadvisable.' Still…I don't know what we'll do about this now…"

We were free from being stuck three mels from the wall, but I had no idea how I'd remove the dangling tail of chain hanging off my wrist now. If we did the same tug-of-war, we could shorten the chain but never remove it entirely.

"I guess we'll just have to lug these everywhere with us. It's a bit heavy, but if you wrap it around your arm, it shouldn't interfere with the ability to run," Eugeo said, doing just that. I followed his lead, and soon we had matching chain gauntlets, which made us smirk at each other.

"So," I said to Eugeo, knowing that we had to clear something up before we moved to the next step, "I need to ask you something, Eugeo. You understand that if we escape and go searching for the truth about Alice, that means open rebellion against the Axiom Church. We don't have time to grapple with what that means, each and every action we take. If that knowledge is too much for you to handle, I think you should stay here."

For the two years we'd known each other, this was probably the hardest thing I'd ever said to him, but it was an unavoidable issue.

He seemed calm on the surface, but Eugeo's fluctlight—his soul as a collection of light quantums—had just experienced a violent restructuring. Ever since birth, he'd believed in the absolute authority of the Axiom Church and Taboo Index. Now he had turned his back on that and placed something else in a higher priority.

I had to assume that Eugeo was in a more unstable position than he seemed, and if I put too much strain on his shifting mental model, it might cause an aberration within his soul like Raios's. That's why I had tried not to mention either the Church or the Index if possible over the last thirty-five hours.

But if we were going to undertake the extreme task of escaping this cell and infiltrating Central Cathedral, I had to get some things straight beforehand so that he didn't have to stop and grapple with a sudden existential quandary in the middle of everything. I had to get Eugeo to the top floor of the cathedral safely—the place where I should find a control console that would let us disengage the simulation and return to reality.

That's right—I wanted to bring my partner and friend out to meet real people in the real world. The Underworld as it existed now was an experiment run by Rath, and they could turn it off or reset it at any time. That would mean deleting the fluctlights of the thousands upon thousands of people who lived in this world. I couldn't let that happen. I needed for Rath, and Seijirou Kikuoka, to have a conversation with Eugeo and realize what they'd built.

The Underworldians weren't just virtual NPCs. They had the same intelligence and emotions as people in the real world, and they had a right to live here.

Eugeo's eyes went wide when I demanded that he prepare for the truth. He lowered his head, lifted his hand, and clenched a fist in front of his chest.

"Yeah...I know." His voice was quiet but resolute, full of determination. "I've made up my mind. I'll turn on the Axiom Church if it means being able to go back to Rulid with Alice. I'll even draw my sword and fight if I have to...If that Integrity Knight is the real Alice, I'll find out what happened to her memory and turn her back. That's what's most important to me."

He looked up, staring at me with absolute resolve shining in his eyes, then grinned faintly. "When we went on that picnic, you said, 'Sometimes there are things that must be done, even when they are forbidden by law.' I feel like I finally understand what that means."

"...I see."

I took a deep breath of cold air to push down the strange feeling I was getting in my chest. I nodded, stepped forward, and patted his shoulder.

"I understand your determination. But...once we're out of here, we're going to avoid battle wherever possible. I don't feel like we stand a chance against any of the other Integrity Knights."

"You're usually not this pessimistic, Kirito." Eugeo smirked. I reminded him that these guys were the toughest fighters in the world, then walked over to the metal bars separating our cell from the hallway. I pulled up the window for one of the three-cen-wide rods. Its object class was 20, and its life was close to ten thousand.

Eugeo came over to look at the window and groaned. "Hmm… that should be easier than the chains, but it'll probably take a while to bend it with our hands. What do you think? Should we body-slam it at the same time?"

"We'll lose plenty of life on our side, too. But I think I've got an idea. Check this out."

I waved him back, then undid the chain wrapped around my right arm. I made it sound like I'd had the idea all along, but in fact, it came to me only when I was first wrapping the chain up. For the first year I'd spent at the Swordcraft Academy, I'd watched my mentor Sortiliena wrap up her own signature leather whip in the exact same way when she was done with it.

Eugeo watched me shake the four-foot-long piece of chain and wondered, "Um, Kirito, are you going to try to break the bar with that? What if you mess up and hit yourself…?"

"Don't worry, I got plenty of lessons in whip-snapping from Liena. They called her the Walking Tactics Manual, remember? Now, if we blow the bars off, it's gonna make a hell of a noise, so we need to run straight for the stairs. Don't fight the jailer if he comes out. Just run."

"…Uh-huh. Plenty of lessons, eh?"

I ignored that and started waving the chain wider and wider. It was still a bit short to use as a proper whip, but that class-38 priority would help make up the gap.

You must strike by focusing on the weight of the tip, not the hand holding the whip, Liena would tell me. I pulled back the chain and, before it stretched all the way out, swung it hard.

"Seya!"

It sprang forward like a dull gray snake, striking the intersection of those thick bars directly and producing a shower of sparks.

Ba-gwaaam! The bar ripped loose from the vertical frame, top and bottom, and slammed into the cell on the far wall with a tremendous clatter. If anyone had been stored in that cell, they would've assumed that Solus had sent down their punishment directly.

I held my breath against the thick cloud of rising dust and tumbled into the hallway. The kettle-headed jailer had to have heard that one. He probably wasn't as tough as an Integrity Knight, but I wasn't going to test that theory with just a length of chain for a weapon.

I crouched and watched the hallway, but after several seconds, there was no change. Eugeo followed me out of the cell. I glanced at him and whispered, "They might be waiting in ambush. Be on your guard."

"Got it."

We started sneaking along to avoid drawing attention—probably a bit too late for that.

According to the information I'd frantically memorized when we were brought down here, the Axiom Church's basement prison had eight hallways that extended outward like wheel spokes, with four cells on either side of each hallway. If all the cells held two at most, that meant it had a maximum capacity of 8 times 8 times 2, or 128 prisoners. I couldn't imagine that it had ever been full, however.

At the "hub" of the wheel where all eight spokes met was the jailer's station, around which wound the spiral staircase that went up to the surface. If we could avoid the jailer's attacks and sprint past him, that would be the best outcome. At the end of the hallway I came to a stop, checking out the area around the station.

There was a small lamp hung on the wall of the rounded station, its light meager and flickering. Nothing at all moved, but I couldn't shake the feeling of the jailer lying in wait somewhere, readying an attack with some terrifying weapon.

"...Hey, Kirito."

"Shh!"

"Uh, Kirito?" Eugeo insisted, tapping my shoulder as I tried to peer around the corner. I turned.

"What?!"

"Do you hear that? Isn't it...snoring?"

"...Uh, what?"

I focused on my ears and heard a rhythmic series of faint but familiar low rumbles.

"..."

I looked at Eugeo again, then shook my head and started walking.

Out of the hallway (without so much as a mouse hiding around the corner, of course), it was a fairly open circular space, with a stone pillar in the center about sixteen feet across. The pillar was hollow inside—the jailer's room—and was, in fact, the source of the snoring.

There was a black metal door on the side of the pillar with a small window in its top. We snuck closer and I pressed my face to the window to look inside.

In the middle of the room was a crude bed, no better than the ones in the cells, with the jailer's barrel-like body spilling over the sides of it. He was still wearing that kettle-like mask, and the thin material vibrated with each snore.

This was our golden opportunity to escape, but I had to wonder about the circumstances of his life. The jailer stood guard over a prison that hardly ever saw any visitors, if I had to guess, and had worked here alone for years, if not decades. After all, unless you were born to a noble family, everyone in this world was given a "calling" at age ten by their local leaders, and there was no way to choose or change it on your own.

Down here in the depths without any sunlight, waking up with the faint sound of the morning bells, patrolling empty cells, then going to sleep to the night bells. This jailer's job had consisted of nothing but that repetition for years and years. An existence so dull and automatic that he hadn't even stirred when we blasted the bars off our cell.

There was a huge array of keys in various sizes hanging on the wall of the station. Somewhere among them would be the keys to our wrist shackles, but I wasn't in the mood to disturb the jailer's sleep and fight him. I stepped back and said, "Let's just go."

"Yeah...I agree."

Eugeo seemed to understand where I was coming from. We moved away from the window and started up the spiral stairs, never looking back.

2

The stairs had felt interminably long when we were descending them, but rushing upward, I sensed the exit was near after just a few minutes. The moldiness of the air trailed away, and the damp stone walls and steps changed to fine, smooth marble.

Eventually the way ahead got lighter, and when the exit came into view, we leaped upward, skipping steps and completely forgetting any sense of caution. Once we were on the surface again, we greedily sucked in lungfuls of fresh air.

"...Ahhh..."

When I felt my respiratory system functioning properly again, I looked around at last. It was dark yet, but the faint amount of starlight was still enough to see by.

The Axiom Church was located on a large square plot of land directly in the middle of Centoria. From what I could see when we were hauled in on the dragon yesterday morning, the main gate was on the east side (probably to face a rising Solus), with a wide approach that led to the church building proper.

That building was the massive, white Central Cathedral. It, too, had a square base, its sheer walls polished to a mirrorlike reflection, and the top was so distant that it was always lost in the clouds and invisible from the ground.

I believed that someone or something at the top of the cathedral managed this world and that someone would maintain a system console that I could use to contact Rath on the outside. If I could just get there, I could return to the real world after two years and two months of being trapped in here…

I turned back to the entrance to the underground stairs, savoring the idea of my potential victory. The doorless, rectangular hole opened rather abruptly in the side of the pure-white building. I looked left, then right, then upward along the smooth, polished marble, but due to the thick fog, I couldn't see a corner in any direction.

Of course, even without the fog, I couldn't have seen the top—that white marble surface was the outside wall of the very cathedral that was my destination.

Following the same train of thought, Eugeo took a few steps forward, raised his hand, and stroked the wall. His fingers rubbed back and forth, ascertaining the absolute solidity and coldness of its surface.

"…I know it shouldn't be a surprise at this point, but…it's hard to believe. We're touching the Central Cathedral itself. Even the greatest nobles—even the four emperors—can only look at this tower from beyond the walls."

"Too bad we're here as escaped fugitives, rather than Integrity Knights like we planned," I deadpanned. Eugeo weakly smiled back for a moment.

"But at this point, it seems like we made the right choice," he said. "What if we became Integrity Knights and turned out like Alice…?"

"With our memories being controlled, you mean? Good point…but if all the knights are like that, I wonder who they think they are," I mused. Eugeo removed his hand from the stone and looked at me.

I put my hand on my hip and explained, "I mean, assuming the knights' memories are being hidden from them…they should at least know things like who their parents are and where they were born, right? I mean, that's the most fundamental root of human experience. I think it would be really hard to fake that kind of knowledge."

"I see…The knights can fly everywhere on those dragons, after all. If you sealed their real memories and gave them fake ones, they could easily go to those locations and realize the lie…"

Suddenly, Eugeo sucked in a deep breath and stared at me. I looked back, surprised at this reaction. After several seconds of staring at each other, I finally recognized the reason for his behavior.

"Oh…you think we might find a way to return my memories in the tower?"

"Er…I—I just…"

He scrunched up his face and looked down at the ground, so I moved toward him and ruffled his flaxen hair. "You're such a worrywart. I told you—whether my memory comes back or not, I'm going along on your journey to the end."

Eugeo raised his reddened faced and protested, "Don't treat me like a child." But he didn't try to brush away my hand. "I'm…I'm not doubting your word. You've said that over and over. But… when I started thinking about how our journey might be coming to an end, it just…"

His voice was tense and thick with emotion, and I started to feel something rising within my own chest. I looked up, hand still on Eugeo's head.

The tremendous monolith standing over us was truly worthy of being called the center of the world. Even if there somehow weren't any obstacles on the way up, the trip would not be easy—but that was all that was left. No matter how many thousands of stairs were between us, once we'd finished climbing them, our journey would be over. And it had taken at least a year less than we had planned.

But this wouldn't be an eternal farewell. I'd log out to the real world, but I would be back. I had to see Eugeo, Liena, Ronie, Tiese, and everyone else again.

"Once it's over, let's make sure we secure a happy ending. You'll get Alice's memories back and take her home to Rulid. But... wouldn't you need to choose a new calling then? You should probably start thinking about that now, because you won't get another chance," I teased.

Eugeo looked up at last, his familiar annoyed expression present. "You're getting way ahead of yourself. But at the very least, I've had enough of cutting down trees."

"Ha-ha, I bet you have."

I took my hand off his head and slapped his shoulder, just as the Bells of Time-Tolling far overhead rang the time, beautiful and grand. That was the four o'clock melody. Only one more hour until daybreak...

"...Looks like we ought to get moving."

"Yeah, let's go."

We knuckled fists in solidarity, the force, timing, and speed of which were perfectly matched. No more words were needed. We set about examining our surroundings again.

For now, all we knew was that we were on the back side of the cathedral, on the west. The eastern side was hidden from view on the other side of the building, of course.

Our present objective was to get inside the cathedral, which would be easy if there were an entrance to the ground floor, but the west face was totally sheer and slippery, with no windows anywhere near low enough to climb up to. The only opening was the staircase exit we had just come out of, and while there just might be other passages back down there, we'd sworn to Stacia that we would never make that trip again.

So the next option was to follow the wall around, either to the north or the south. The problem was that less than twenty feet in either direction, there were metal fences flush against the building wall. They were low enough to climb over with some difficulty, but I'd seen during the flight in yesterday that there were actually many fences arrayed in rows.

Based on the well-burnished look of the bronze fences covered in vines, they were probably tougher than the bars down in the cells. There were layers upon layers of these impediments on the west side of the cathedral. It was a garden as much as it was a maze—most likely to keep in any prisoners in the unlikely event of an escape.

So between the wall and fences, the east, south, and north were blocked, but there was a gate to the west. Beyond it was a short, straight path that led to a clearing in the maze. That was where the dragon had landed yesterday.

Just before that had happened, I had tried to memorize the escape route, but the maze was so complex and my time so brief that it was completely impossible. Now it seemed we didn't have any other option.

"We've got to make our way through the maze…and reach the north or south side of the cathedral," I said.

Eugeo agreed. "I put my hope on your instincts."

"I've got this. Always been good at mazes," I replied without thinking. Eugeo gave me a strange look, and I had to start walking before he asked me how I would know that.

Within a few paces, we were at the gate to the west; I opened the window of the metal fence to check its priority level. The window said it was 35—as I suspected, it was special bronze. I could break it in a number of swings with the chain around my right hand, but not only would it take longer than climbing, it was likely to attract the attention of the guards or even an Integrity Knight.

We were about to resume our attempt on the maze as originally planned when Eugeo gasped.

"Wh-what is it? Is it something about the fence?!" I asked.

"N-no, not the fence…These leaves…"

Eugeo was staring at the vine wrapped around the fence, pointing out a plain old leaf growing on it.

"I've never seen one, but I'm certain…it's a *rose*, Kirito."

"A rose, huh…? Wait, really?! All these plants growing in the maze…?!"

It hadn't seemed significant at first, but then I remembered that roses were no ordinary flowers in the Underworld. The Four Holy

Flowers—anemones, marigolds, dahlias, and cattleyas—all grew fruit that contained very high-purity sacred power. But even more valuable was the rose, the Flower of the Gods. Commoners, nobles, and emperors alike were forbidden to cultivate them. The few that grew naturally in some remote mountains were worth a fortune at the markets of Centoria.

And there were thousands, tens of thousands of them just in this maze…I was overcome with a sudden urge to go pick as many as I could find, but sadly, the Underworld didn't have a handy inventory system to hide them in.

In contrast to my baser instincts, Eugeo's reaction was quite calm. He pulled apart the jagged-edged leaves and peered deeper into the growth.

"The flowers aren't blooming yet, but you can see the buds swelling. With this many of them, I'm sure they put off an extreme amount of spatial power."

Now that he mentioned it, the air in the maze was sweet and rich, and every breath felt like it was purifying me. I inhaled and exhaled greedily, but Eugeo just looked annoyed.

"No, what I mean is, we might be able to use higher sacred arts here."

"…That's great, but we're not injured or anything…"

"True, but we *are* missing something very important. Our…"

"Oh, r-right! Our swords!" I said, finally realizing what Eugeo was getting at, and snapped my fingers. Our class-38 whip-chains were powerful weapons, but Eugeo didn't know how to use one, so the sooner we got the Blue Rose Sword and the Black One back, the better. In fact, it should be our top priority.

We hadn't seen the swords since Alice the Integrity Knight took them away, but with the help of sacred arts, we could form a good guess as to their location. I raised my right hand, took a deep breath, and said, "System Call!"

To Eugeo, this was the initiation of a magical spell. To me, it was a system control command. Purple light gathered faintly around our fingers, signaling that the booted command prompt was ready. I extended my index finger and squeezed the other four before delivering the next command.

"Generate Umbra Element!"

As I chanted, I envisioned a gemstone, black and matte, and on the tip of my finger appeared a tiny orb, totally black with blue and purple highlights. This was a darkness element, one of the eight kinds in this world. On the overall scale, it was a difficult spell, but at least those boring sacred arts classes and tests had carried over to practical use.

Darkness elements were the opposite of the light elements that Miss Azurica had used to heal Eugeo's eye—they had a negative energy to them. They were dangerous: If discharged, they could easily scoop out and empty the surrounding space. But their adhesive properties were equally useful.

"Adhere Possession. Object ID WLSS102382. Discharge." I finished chanting, and the floating element began to move away, as if drawn by a magnet. The orb wobbled and rose as it moved east, until it ran out of energy just before the cathedral wall and vanished. For several seconds, it left behind a faint blue-purple trail that hung in the air.

I watched it closely, following the trajectory of the line. Eugeo did the same and murmured, "As I was afraid. They're inside the cathedral. I was hoping they'd been stashed in some kind of storage shed outside..."

"But it doesn't seem like they're very high inside the building. Only the second floor...maybe the third. That's better than if they'd been carried way higher."

"Yeah...I guess. Then let's set our sights on sneaking into the cathedral using some method other than the front door and head for the third floor to retrieve our swords."

At the academy, I was the only one who'd dare to say things like *sneak into* and *retrieve*, but now Eugeo was getting into the game. I wasn't sure if that was a good thing or not, but that wasn't important now.

We knew where to find the swords, but it hadn't changed the

situation with the rose maze. If only I could cast a sacred art that would display the path to the exit, but there were no commands *that* convenient here—I thought.

Eugeo and I passed through the bronze gate again and headed for the little clearing straight ahead. If the roses were blooming in the daytime, it would make for a gorgeous sight, but the darkness was our friend for now. We continued stealthily but quickly under the light of the stars.

The next gate soon made its appearance. Just past it was the clearing where the dragon landed. I recalled seeing benches and a small fountain, but I wasn't sure if there was a map of the garden as well. But it was a clearing for general use, so there should be one. There must be!

Just as we passed through the second, smaller gate, I felt a familiar pain at the roots of my bangs, while Eugeo tugged on the back of my coat.

"Wh-what?"

"…Someone's here."

"What…?"

I tensed and peered forward.

The clearing was rectangular, elongated east to west, with the gate at the eastern end. In the center was a fountain with a bronze statue of Terraria, surrounded by four benches of the same metal as the fences.

And just as Eugeo said, on the northern bench—the right-hand one, from our perspective—was a figure.

The face was hidden behind long, flowing hair. The person's slender form was clad in polished silver armor and carried a curved longsword on the left side. Hanging from the shoulders was a dark-colored cape. Even from here, the circled cross insignia was clear.

"An…Integrity Knight…"

There was no question. Based on size, hair, and color, it was not Alice, but it *was* clear that this knight was just as powerful as

she. This was not a foe who could be beaten without a sword...
perhaps not even *with* our weapons.

We had to rush into the maze, either to the north or south. Or
perhaps turn back, I considered. But before I could even make a
decision, a pleasant male voice sounded through the clearing.

"Don't just stand there. Come in, prisoners."

There was a shining object in his hand. To my surprise, it was
a wineglass. There was a bottle sitting next to him on the bench.

I sensed something confrontational about this, and yet I
couldn't help but indulge my bad habit of rising to the bait.

"What, are you going to serve us some wine?"

The knight didn't answer right away. He looked over at us and
motioned with the glass.

"Sadly, this is not for children like you...especially not criminal children. It's a hundred-and-fifty-year vintage from the
Western Empire. I might let you sample its bouquet, though." He
grinned, swiveling the glass in his fingers. Even in the starlight,
he was shockingly handsome. The combination of his promi-
nent, thin-bridged nose and slightly wild eyebrows had a pro-
found balance, and his long, sharp eyes glinted with intelligence.

Eugeo and I were both shocked into silence. The knight
uncrossed his legs and stood up, his armor faintly ringing. He
was very tall—at least a head taller than me. His deep-violet cape
and pale-purple hair both flowed in the night breeze.

The man took a sip of his wine and caught me off guard when
he said, "I must admire my teacher Alice's wisdom. She perfectly
predicted this most unlikely prison break."

"Alice...your teacher...?" I repeated.

The knight nodded easily and continued, "She ordered me
to spend the night out here in case you escaped, but I honestly
thought it was preposterous. I planned to gaze at the rosebuds
and nurse a bottle of wine through the night, but here you are,
in the flesh. Those chains wrapped around your arms are made
of spiristeel forged in the volcanoes of the Southern Empire.

I don't know how you cut them, but it's clear now that you have no regard for the law."

He smiled and set the wineglass on the bench, then ran his free hand through his hair and continued, "I'll be returning you to the cells, of course, but before that, you ought to be punished. I assume you understand that."

His thin smile hadn't left, but there was power radiating from his tall, lean form, and I had to resist the urge to falter. I summoned what strength I could muster to reply, "Then *I* assume you know we aren't going to submit to your punishment without a fight."

"Ha-ha-ha! Very feisty. I'd heard you were just pups who hadn't even graduated the academy, but I'm impressed. In honor of your empty threat, I will give you my name, before I beat you to the last shred of your life. I am the Integrity Knight Eldrie Synthesis Thirty-One. I was freshly summoned just a month ago, and I don't have any territory to my name yet—hope you don't mind that."

When this speech was over, Eugeo sighed over my shoulder, but I didn't pay attention—because there had been several crucial bits of information contained in that annoyingly smooth introduction.

First of all, this established a clear rule to the naming of the Integrity Knights. Alice's full name was Alice Synthesis Thirty, so it was clear that Alice and Eldrie were their personal names. The *Synthesis* in the middle was commonly shared. And the last name was just a number. Eugeo wouldn't have understood, because they were *English* numbers, but it would suggest that Alice was the thirtieth of the knights, while Eldrie was the thirty-first.

He also said that he was "summoned just a month ago." I wasn't sure what he meant by summoned, exactly, but if he was indeed the newest of the knights, that meant there were only thirty-one of them in total. And given that many of them had to leave Central Cathedral to protect the various regions of the human empire, that meant there couldn't be more than twenty in the tower itself.

But all that calculation was putting the cart before the horse if we couldn't defeat the newest and greenest of the knights.

I turned my head and hissed to Eugeo, who stood behind me, "We're going to fight. I'll go first. You wait for my signal."

"O-okay. But…Kirito, I…"

"I told you, there's no time to hesitate anymore. If we can't beat him, there's no way we'll get up to the cathedral."

"Um, I'm not hesitating, I'm saying that his name is— Oh, never mind. It can wait. But don't be too reckless, Kirito."

Based on his reaction, I wasn't sure if Eugeo had understood the full plan, but we didn't have time to hold a strategy meeting. I got the feeling that my invisible guardian spirit above my head sighed, but we could still flee for safety after ascertaining the enemy's strength—I hoped.

I took two steps forward through the gate, then unraveled the chain and held it in my fingers. The knight noticed this and raised his eyebrow in curiosity.

"I see. I wondered how you would fight without a sword. A chain, eh? I suppose it might end up being a proper battle after all."

His voice and expression were still overflowing with confidence. I inched closer, swearing under my breath that I'd wipe the smugness off his features soon enough.

The chain had a handicap: I couldn't use my special sword skills with it. But it had much longer reach than a sword. If I kept moving, striking and disengaging, it should eventually build up enough damage to give us a chance.

It took one moment for that ray of hope to be smashed to pieces. Eldrie reached not for his sword but behind his back, and he said, "Then I shall forego my sword and use this."

When his right hand emerged, it held a second weapon he had concealed under his cape—a thin whip that shone silver.

As I watched in disbelief, Eldrie let the whip hang so that it coiled on the stones like a snake. Unlike my crude chain, the weapon was of finely woven silver cords. And upon closer look, there were fine spiraling spikes running down its length like rose thorns, glinting wickedly in the starlight. It would do more than tear the skin if it hit me.

On top of that, it was at least a dozen feet long, at least three times the length of my chain. My plan to strike and keep my distance was ruined.

I froze, feeling a cold sweat break out. Eldrie noted the change and snapped his hand. The whip leaped like a living thing, cracking on the stone ground.

"And now...in recognition and admiration of your rebellion against the Axiom Church's Taboo Index and your escape from imprisonment, I will do you the honor of fighting my hardest from the word *go.*"

Before I could react, Eldrie switched the whip from right hand to left and shouted, "System Call!"

The exceedingly complex commands he gave were too fast for me to make out.

The sacred arts of the Underworld were like the magic system of *ALfheim Online* in that high-speed casting was possible—in other words, saying the commands as quickly as you could. But the faster you tried to chant, the greater the likelihood you would flub a word and screw up.

Of the people I knew, the second-best at high-speed chanting was Sortiliena, with the best being Miss Azurica. But Eldrie spoke even faster than her. He finished the thirty-plus-word command in barely seven or eight seconds, finishing with an unfamiliar phrase.

"...Enhance Armament!"

I understood the English word *enhance*, fortunately. But *armament*...?

He didn't give me time to consult my mental dictionary. Eldrie lazily raised his arm, pointed it at me, then swung.

The distance between us was a good fifty feet. No matter how long his whip was, it couldn't reach. And yet.

Eldrie's whip left a silver trail in the air as it stretched several times its actual length, as though made of some elastic material. Even in my shock, I lifted my chain with both hands overhead on instinct. There was a tremendous blast, and pale-white sparks showered down around me.

"Urgh...!"

My instincts told me that if I took the blow standing still, it would sever my chain. I bent my knees and twisted to the right to deflect the whip to the side. It scraped nastily along the metal and flew past to strike the stone ground, where it left a deep groove before returning to the knight's hand.

Another wave of cold sweat rushed from my pores as I looked at my chain and groaned. The blow had gouged the class-38 object made of "spiristeel," whatever that was, to the point that one of the rings was nearly ready to split apart.

The Integrity Knight smirked at my shock and remarked, "Well, well...I was expecting to take off your ear, but you managed to evade my divine Frostscale Whip at first glance. I suppose I should apologize for assuming you were a mere student."

I really wanted to deliver a good comeback to that cocky comment, but my mouth refused to move.

He was powerful. He was deadly. If anyone was unconsciously underestimating the other, it was me. Eldrie Synthesis Thirty-One was a type of foe I'd never faced before, I belatedly realized.

The Underworld was Rath's virtual-reality experiment, so in a strict sense, there was no mortal danger to me, Kazuto Kirigaya. If Eldrie's whip knocked my head off and reduced my life to zero, it wouldn't harm my actual flesh in the least.

So in a certain sense, the fear involved in battle wasn't the same as in *SAO*, the game of death. Facing enormous floor bosses or psychotic red players in Aincrad, having that tightrope sense of the yawning abyss just beneath your feet—that was a sensation I'd never feel again, and I was glad for it.

Yet that game of death was populated with online gamers like me, who had no real knowledge of swordfighting. We were risking our lives based on stats and numbers, physical motion assistance systems, and reaction speeds honed over a year or two of practice at best.

But Eldrie was different. He'd spent more than a decade of his life in this world training and disciplining his skills, perfecting his craft to its limit. He was a true warrior, physically and mentally. He wasn't an *SAO* player or a monster under the server's control. He was a rune knight from a fantasy novel come to life.

Eldrie had sharper skills and sacred arts than the goblins we fought in the cave under the End Mountains. His willpower was stronger than even the first-seat elite disciples Raios Antinous and Volo Levantein. He likely had the advantage over me in every possible way. If I fought him with nothing more than a single metal chain, I was 100 percent going to lose.

If there was anything I could use to get out of this situation, it was...

You are not alone.

For a second, it felt like someone had spoken my own thought aloud. Following that instinct, I whispered to my partner, "Eugeo, the only way we can win is because there's two of us. I'll try to stop his whip. Then you hit him."

I didn't hear a response. When I quickly snuck a look over my shoulder, I saw that it wasn't fear on Eugeo's face but admiration. When he did eventually speak, my suspicions were confirmed.

"Did you see that sacred art, Kirito? That was incredible...I've only read about it in an old book at the library, but I recognize it. That was Perfect Weapon Control...an ultrahigh-level art that works on the very matter of your weapon and uses a divine miracle to increase the weapon's strength. No wonder he's an Integrity Knight!"

"This isn't the time for gushing, man! Anyway, if that helps increase the attack span, do you think that Perfect Control would work on our chains, too?"

"No way! That's a top-level secret art, according to the Church. And it only works on divine-level weapons."

"Then we'll have to forget about that one and make do with what we've got on hand. Anyway, I'll find a way to stop his whip, and you finish him off. I know you're not used to whips, but you can at least swing it downward, right?"

Eugeo finally got his face under control again, and I warned him, "You've gotta be ready, remember? He's an Integrity Knight, the highest force of the Axiom Church—and we've got to beat him."

"...I know. I told you, I won't lose sight of the goal," Eugeo answered, and used his free hand to loosen the chain wrapped around his arm, too. We looked forward again, where the knight smiled his cool smile and snapped his silver whip.

"Done with your little strategy meeting, prisoners? I hope you've come up with something fun."

"...Should an Integrity Knight really be playing with fire like that?"

"It's correct that we must mete out divine justice on those who rebel against the Church. That is the will of our exalted pontifex. But as a proud knight, it pains me to lash the weak and helpless with my whip. So I am holding out hope that you are at least strong enough to put a scratch on my armor and prove your worth as foes."

"Scratch your armor? We'll knock off half your life, and your cocky smile with it." I snarled to hide the rising panic inside me. The "pontifex" Eldrie mentioned was an interesting title, but I didn't have time to contemplate the implications. I gave my chain a wave, then thrust out my left hand at Eldrie.

"System Call! Generate Thermal Element!" I commanded, imagining a crimson ruby. Glowing red orbs grew at the end of my thumb, index, and middle fingers. They were flame elements, the basis for fire-based attack spells. I was going to continue, but Eldrie calmly held up his hand in response.

"System Call. Generate Cryogenic Element."

Those were blue ice elements to counteract my fire, and there were five, one for each finger. He already had the advantage of numbers, but I ignored that and continued, "Flame Element, Arrow Shape!"

I opened my left hand, stretching out the lights so that they turned into three flaming arrows. They were designed for maximum speed and puncturing power. As quickly as I could, so as not to give the enemy time to react, I chanted, "Fly Straight! Discharge!"

A vortex of flame erupted, and the trio of arrows shot toward Eldrie.

In a world where sword battle was the orthodox method of combat, attack-type sacred arts existed only to battle the forces of darkness—or so the old lecturer at the academy said. He'd probably have a stroke if he knew I was using his lessons to attack an Integrity Knight.

I leaped forward after the arrows. Up ahead, Eldrie chanted a counteracting art in one breath.

"Form Element, Bird Shape. Counter Thermal Object, Discharge!"

The five blue dots turned into little birds—ideal for homing—that took flight at once. My arrows were faster, but there were more of the little ice birds. The fiery shafts slipped past two of them, but the other three pounced on the arrows, causing the flames and ice crystals to shatter and cancel each other out. The force of the collisions knocked the wineglass off the bench, and it shattered on the stones.

I bore down on Eldrie, using the flashy explosion as cover. Two steps until I was within my chain range…One step…

The knight's right hand snapped, and the silver whip leaped off the ground like a snake. At this range, his Perfect Weapon Control range boost was meaningless. I watched it curve in from the right and tried to read its path, tilting my body to avoid it so I could cross that last step. But—

"—?!"

My breath caught in my throat. Eldrie's whip split into two in midair, the new silver snake cutting a sharper angle to bear down on me directly.

I was already trying to avoid the original blow by inches, and I had no way to dodge this one. The whip struck me right in the chest and slammed me down onto the cobblestones.

"Gaahh!"

I'd been expecting it, but even then, the pain of those countless metal thorns on the whip made my vision briefly go dark. I clenched my teeth and looked down to see that the chest part of my black uniform had torn through both layers, with a vivid red line running across the exposed skin beneath it. Little drops of blood began to form along its length and trickle downward in parallel lines as they oozed forth.

Eldrie looked at me, splayed out on the stones, and laughed heartily.

"Ha-ha-ha! Those tricks won't work on the Frostscale Whip. When under Perfect Control, not only can it cover up to fifty mels, it can also split into up to seven parts. If there were eight of you, then you might stand a chance attacking me all at once."

I didn't have the mind to get angry this time. I hadn't experienced such searing pain since the goblin captain hit my shoulder two years ago.

I always tried to remember that my lack of resistance to pain was one of my greatest weaknesses here, but given that the stop-short rule was practiced in almost all cases at the academy, I just hadn't had the chance to build up my hardiness. I talked a big game about stopping the whip with my body, but this result was pathetic.

"Uh-oh, did I put too much hope in you? Well, I can be merciful and at least knock you out quickly," Eldrie boasted. He took a step forward, silver armor scraping.

Just then, Eugeo leaped out from behind the fountain, sheer desperation on his features. *"Uraaah!"*

With a rare bellow, he swung down his chain. It was a tremendous swing for someone with no experience using one, and it came with perfect timing—but it still wasn't enough to break the knight's defenses.

Eldrie's right hand moved at blurring speed, the silver whip splitting once again. One of the tendrils deflected the chain, and the other hit Eugeo. Like me, it hit him on the chest, and he was thrown into the fountain with a huge splash before he could even react.

The shocking pain of my wound was still vivid, but I couldn't waste the opportunity that Eugeo's suicide attack had created. Sensing that Eldrie's attention was mostly focused away from me, I sat up and hurled what I'd had clenched in my right hand at the knight's face.

Unlike in Aincrad and Alfheim, in this world, most objects did not immediately vanish when they were destroyed. Pieces, fragments, even corpses received their own fresh, new life-counter.

That life—its durability—would dwindle much faster than it had before breaking, and once down to zero, it would crumble without a trace for good. But even then, it usually took a few minutes to get there.

Even for fragile little things like broken wineglasses.

The shard of glass cut through the predawn night toward Eldrie's left eye. I'd even rubbed some of my blood on it before I threw it, so it wouldn't reflect the light of the stars.

It didn't take a tenth of a second from the moment it entered his view until it struck. But even then, the knight had the reaction speed to turn his face to the right and avoid a direct hit on his eye. The piece of glass scratched his left cheekbone and disappeared into the darkness, leaving only a shallow cut.

"Whoa!!"

I was in a squat before Eldrie could turn back to face me, and I raced forward. Two steps later, I was in chain range. I pulled it back over my left shoulder in preparation to strike. Momentarily startled, Eldrie recovered and brought his right hand back, returning the whip from its attack on Eugeo to use it against me.

If I just crudely swung the chain forward, the weapons would clash at best, or the whip would split and hit just me again at worst. But I banished my fear and focused hard on the gleaming end of the whip—then on the spot behind Eldrie, where Eugeo had fallen into the fountain.

In every style of swordfighting we learned about at the Sword-craft Academy, it was a tremendous mistake to take your eye off an enemy during an attack. A kind of "taboo," in fact. Swordsmen in this world would never do that. Even Integrity Knights.

"*Hrng!*"

And thus Eldrie grunted and, for an instant, turned his focus away from me. He sensed that Eugeo was instantly going to rise from the fountain after his fall, striving to attack again. But that was a sensation he received only because I shifted my eyes away from him. Eugeo was tough, but not enough to take a hit from a Divine Object and get up the next second.

Mirroring Eldrie's hesitation, his silver whip wavered briefly in midair. It passed my chain, missing by just a hair. I'd chosen the awkward backhand from the left to make the chain run parallel to the whips and increase the difficulty of deflection—a trick I'd learned through hard experience with my wooden sword against Liena's whip.

But this strategy wouldn't work twice. It was my one, only, final chance.

"*Zeyaaaaah!!*"

I screamed with all my soul and swung down the spiristeel chain with all my strength.

My aim was at his head, the only part of the knight's body not protected by that shining armor. Whether he'd taken his helmet off to drink the wine or had assumed he simply wouldn't need it against mere students, I wasn't going to let that chance pass. A good heavy chain smashing an unprotected head could even knock out an Integrity Knight, I bet...

But once again, Eldrie displayed an ability I never considered.

His left hand shot out like lightning and caught the end of the chain—not with the gauntlet armor on the back of his hand but with the thin leather glove of his palm.

If he'd taken it with the back of his hand, the chain would have wrapped around the point like a fulcrum and still hit his head, albeit not as powerfully. In that sense, Eldrie made the right choice—but that thin leather glove wasn't going to absorb a blow from a class-38 chain.

"*Urgh...!*"

He grunted, unable to conceal his pain. I clearly heard the sound of multiple bones in his left hand breaking all at once. He wouldn't be able to use that hand for a while, and I didn't think him likely to toss aside that Frostscale Whip for a different weapon.

I'd leap on him and start a hand-to-hand fight. Liena had taught me some of the Serlut style's martial arts. It was more suited to holds than blows, but against a heavily armored opponent, that was actually a good thing.

"Not done yet!" I shouted, and lunged forward, ready to use my left hand to grab his injured arm.

"I don't think so!"

But the thirty-first and newest Integrity Knight once again betrayed my expectations. He squeezed the chain with his broken hand and pulled. The chain was rooted to the shackle around my right wrist, so it pulled me in the opposite rotation and threw off my balance. I desperately tried to hold my ground, but Eldrie bellowed and attempted to swing me away.

"*Hrrng!!*"

If he succeeded, I'd be out of my chain's range and back on the wrong end of his whip. He'd ensure I didn't get close again.

On instinct, I adjusted my left hand's target from Eldrie's left arm to the right hand holding his weapon. The Frostscale Whip's many thorns did not reach down to the last four feet or so from its handle. I wrapped that part of it around my arm so that it couldn't break free.

Unless Eldrie let go of both his whip and my chain, he couldn't put distance between us. If he released my chain, I could wail on him all I wanted. He sensed that, too, so he gripped my weapon even harder in his crushed hand.

This stalemate of steel chain and silver whip kept us just over three feet apart. I was sure his broken hand had to be screaming in pain as it clutched the chain, but the knight showed no signs of it on his face.

"I suppose I must take back my statement about expecting too much of you. I never thought I would be pushed this hard," he murmured, still calm and cool.

"Gee, thanks," I said, wishing that I could have given him a snappier comeback—but I didn't want to draw attention to our wounds. Between Eldrie's fractured hand and my chest lacerations, the bleeding whip wound was making my life descend faster. If he realized this, he could maintain his hold on my chain and wait until I started to weaken.

But perhaps he already knew. The knight smiled, but if his next statement was meant to buy him more time, it was an odd way of doing it.

"You know, that way you fight...I feel like I've seen it before, strangely enough."

"Oh yeah? It shouldn't be that strange. Maybe you've fought someone else who uses the Serlut style before?"

"Hah. That's not possible, prisoner. I told you, I was summoned into the human realm as an Integrity Knight only a month ago."

"...When you say 'summoned'..." I started to ask, but then I heard the sound. Or more accurately, I heard a shift in a sound that was already there.

In the middle of the fountain behind Eldrie was the stone statue of Terraria, the deity of earth. The statue held a little jug that was pouring a constant trickle of water into the fountain below—but now the sound was muffled. It was a sign. From my partner to me.

Eldrie would notice it soon, too. I had to keep up the conversation and be ready to move.

"...that makes it sound like someone snapped their fingers and called you here."

In order to distract him, I had to do something. But releasing the Frostscale Whip from my arm wasn't an option. That left only one possibility...

I yanked hard on the chain!

Eldrie reacted by pulling back to return the position to equilibrium. The metal yanked tight, and almost immediately, the chain snapped down the middle. The piece that had taken the whip blow moments earlier finally gave out.

"Wha—!" He gasped and lost his balance.

It was then that Eugeo leaped out of the fountain with a huge splash. He'd recovered from the blow to his chest and was waiting beneath the statue's trickle for his chance to attack. The change in sound had come from the flow of water striking his back.

"*Raaaah!!*"

Eugeo swung his chain down at Eldrie's defenseless head, spraying water droplets everywhere. But half a second before that, the knight had spoken a brief command.

"Release Recollection."

This phrase, I didn't understand at all. But the effect it had, given the brevity of the command itself, was so impossible, it seemed to transcend the category of sacred arts.

The silver whip wrapped around my left hand, so tight that he could neither push nor pull it away, flashed brightly. Then it began thrashing around like a living animal—and extended tremendously fast.

The Frostscale Whip, now a shining snake, soared over our heads and leaped onto the chain in Eugeo's hand. And "snake" wasn't just a bit of poetic license. On the tip of the whip, I saw little ruby eyes and bared fangs.

The snake bit down on the end of the chain, pulled it (and Eugeo) up into the air, and slammed it down onto the cobblestones just next to me. Eugeo landed on his back and grunted. That added up to more damage for him than me so far, but he valiantly attempted to rise again.

But a ferociously sharp tip grazed his wet bangs before he could get up.

Eldrie had recovered his balance, tossed aside the broken chain, and pulled his sword free to point it at Eugeo. It was a thin blade, but it shone with the richness of a fine make. The weight of it had to be killing the broken bones of his left hand, but there was only the faintest hint of a furrow between his eyebrows.

The silver snake, which—for all I could tell—had protected its master of its own accord, shriveled up and returned to being a plain old whip again. Whatever that Release Recollection command was, its miracle had a short time limit.

The situation was in a stalemate at last.

I had Eldrie's whip stuck to my hand. I'd lost half my chain. Eugeo had a sword to his face, keeping him still. Eldrie seemed to have the advantage, being the one with the sword, but I doubted he could do all that much with it, given the state of his hand.

Silence settled upon the little rose garden in the predawn chill.

It was Eldrie who spoke first again. "No wonder Alice was worried about you. You attack without form or pattern…but I suppose that succeeded at catching me off guard. I can't believe you forced me to use my Memory Release skill."

"Memory…?" I repeated. Then I finally understood the meaning of that mysterious command. "Recollection" was a synonym for memory. So it was a sacred art that unleashed the memories… of the weapon?

Memories of the weapon. That sounded familiar from the recent past, and I was about to consult my own memories when Eugeo gasped with admiration for some reason. He said, "And you…are every bit as great as I imagined, Sir Knight."

"Th-this isn't the moment for compliments! And…what do you mean, 'as you imagined'?" I couldn't help but reply. He made it sound like he'd known this knight before.

"I thought the name sounded familiar when he said it. And now I remember. Kirito, this man is the Norlangarth Empire's champion swordsman for this year...as well as *the winner of the Quad-Empire Unification Tournament—Eldrie Woolsburg!*"

"Wha...?"

I stared at the Integrity Knight standing two paces away.

The Northern Empire's champion. That meant he won the Imperial Battle Tournament held in late March. He was the representative of the Imperial Knights, the man who defeated Sortiliena in the first round and Volo Levantein in the second. He won the Quad-Empire Unification Tournament in early April with overwhelming skill, making him this year's greatest swordsman in the human empire and earning him an invitation to Central Cathedral.

I now realized that I didn't know that mighty warrior's name. There was no Internet in this world, no television or radio, so the only form of news media was the primitive "town square" type of weekly newspaper displayed for the public. I hadn't been bothered to go check out the school's bulletin board, but apparently Eugeo had faithfully read it every week.

"You're such an honor student," I grumbled—I couldn't help myself. But if Eugeo was right, and this Eldrie Synthesis Thirty-One was indeed this year's champion, Eldrie Woolsburg, then something about his actions didn't add up.

Eldrie had said that he was summoned to the human realm as an Integrity Knight one month ago. I would understand if he were *designated* an Integrity Knight...but he made it sound like...

"...What...did you...?"

That hoarse whisper didn't come from me. I looked away from my partner back at the knight.

For some reason, Eldrie was pale, his faintly purplish gray eyes wide as if grappling with some monumental shock to the system. His bloodless lips trembled and formed the words, "I was... Northern...Champion...? Eldrie...Woolsburg...?"

Eugeo was taken aback by this puzzling reaction. But he recovered, closed his mouth, and said, "Th-that's right. It said so in the newspaper last month. A handsome man with purple hair…who won every match by landing a perfectly clean hit with his graceful, flowing style…"

"No…I…I'm the Integrity Knight Eldrie Synthesis Thirty-One! I…I've never heard the name Woolsburg!"

I interjected, briefly forgetting that we were in the middle of a fight. "B-but you weren't *born* an Integrity Knight. Wasn't that just your name before you were designated a knight…?"

"I don't know! I…I've never heard it!!" he wailed, hair flying. His face was white as a ghost now, eyes rolling and twitching. "I…I received…the summons of the pontifex, the administrator…and was brought here from the heavens as an Integrity Kni—"

He stopped abruptly.

And then something even more shocking happened.

A purple line of light appeared right in the center of Eldrie's smooth forehead.

"Grgh…uhhh…"

All the strength went out of his hand, but I was too busy staring at his head to think of wresting the whip away from him. The glowing line formed a small, inverted triangle. It wasn't just a magical seal, it was floating further and further out of his brow. The clear triangular pillar, like some kind of crystal, jutted out an inch or two from his skin, flashing and shining.

Inside the prism, fine tendrils of light ran freely in every direction. Once it had extended to a few inches, the whip and sword tumbled out of Eldrie's hands.

His eyes were vacant. He stumbled backward a few steps, then fell to his knees like a lifeless puppet. The crystal on his forehead flashed and pulsed, and I could hear a strange ringing sound from it.

If I'm going to act, it has to be now, I decided, but I didn't have a clue what that action should be.

Attacking would be easy: I'd pick his sword up off the ground and strike it against his defenseless neck. That wouldn't just incapacitate him, it would kill him.

We could also run for our lives. If we somehow jolted the knight back to his senses, I felt like he'd truly go for the jugular. Our sneak attacks wouldn't work, and we might be the ones facing impending death.

Lastly, and perhaps riskiest of all: We could stand here and watch what happened.

Whatever I was seeing now had something to do with the root of the Integrity Knights and the Axiom Church's secrets. Why had Alice lost her memory and turned into someone else? Why did Eldrie talk about summoning? Perhaps I would know the answers if I watched this phenomenon to the end.

And for one thing, Eugeo would not be happy if I attacked Eldrie while he was helpless like this. We weren't guaranteed to find the exit of the rose maze if we ran, either. We had to brave danger and continue watching.

I was inching closer to the kneeling Integrity Knight when the jutting triangular prism blinked, then began to recede back into his head.

"*Ugh...*"

I bit my lip. I'd been hoping that the prism would fall out entirely and cause some kind of event.

"Eldrie! Eldrie Woolsburg!" I shouted. The crystal paused for an instant, then continued moving again. His old name alone wouldn't be enough to complete whatever this process was. I needed a more definitive memory.

I turned to Eugeo, who was watching the display in disbelief, and hissed, "Eugeo, is there anything else you know about Eldrie?! Anything at all—we need to stimulate his memories!"

"Um..." He squinted briefly, then nodded. "Eldrie! You are the son of General Eschdor Woolsburg of the Imperial Knights! Your mother's name is...El...Al...Oh! Almera!"

"..."

The blank-faced knight's lips trembled slightly.

"Al...me...ra..." he croaked, and the prism shone brightly. But even more surprising to me were the large tears that fell from his bulging eyes. Again, he wheezed, "M…Moth…er…"

"That's right…remember! All of it!" I commanded, stepping closer.

But I couldn't approach farther.

A heavy thud rumbled the ground, causing me to pitch forward. I didn't even feel the stomach-churning pain until I looked down and saw the arrow sunk deep into the top of my right foot.

"Aaagh!" I cried, unable to hold it in. I grabbed the dark-red arrow, moaning, and pulled it right out. The pain redoubled as I did, but I somehow managed to keep myself from fainting.

"Kirito! A-are you all—" Eugeo started to say, but I grabbed the end of his dangling chain and hurled him downward.

Fwupp, fwupp! Two arrows stood in the ground right where Eugeo had been. I tugged him farther away, still holding the chain, and looked up into the sky.

Against the stars, starting to fade in the first hints of dawn to the east, I saw a dragon in flight, turning slowly. If I squinted, I could make out a figure in the saddle on its back. It was clearly an Integrity Knight, but if they were able to hit us with a bow at that distance, while riding a mount, they were one hell of a sharpshooter.

The knight drew back their massive bow, and I pushed off the ground with my injured foot as hard as I could. Again, two arrows thudded into the stones right before me.

"Uh, th-this is bad," I stammered, still holding Eugeo's chain. I'd never taken a blow from an arrow here before. Even Sortiliena, the Walking Tactics Manual, had only ever faced throwing daggers, so I had assumed that ranged weapons were not to the liking of the Underworld's warriors. But it seemed that anything went when it came to the Integrity Knights.

I had to envision the area around us because I couldn't take my eyes off the dragon, but as far as I recalled, there was no cover that could hide us here. Not even the leaves of the rose plants on the fences would completely hide us. That left only…

"We've got to run! Dodge the next shot, then sprint!" I whispered to Eugeo, waiting tensely for the next volley.

But this new knight stopped there and had the dragon descend. Within moments, the knight's booming voice filled the fountain clearing.

"Criminals, move away from Knight Thirty-One!"

Against my better judgment, I glanced back at Eldrie and saw that after all the work we'd done, his prism was receding back into his forehead.

"There shall be no forgiveness for the crime of tempting a bright and noble Integrity Knight into ruin! I will pin you down, limb by limb, and cast you into the cells myself!"

Just then, a ray of sunlight from the east caught the dragon. The rider wore heavy silver armor much like Eldrie's and held a massive red longbow in his left hand; it was probably another Divine Object like the Frostscale Whip. The most pressing question was its tremendous accuracy: Was that the effect of its Perfect Control, or had I not even seen its true power yet?

The large knight nocked four arrows to his crimson bow.

"Uh...run!"

He was too close now for us to evade after he loosed the arrows. I started sprinting with Eugeo's chain still in my hand. My chest and right foot throbbed powerfully with each step, but I couldn't stop now. Eugeo kept up behind me, breathing wildly.

I considered running back down to the cells, but that would only shelter us from the arrows, not solve our problem. We rushed through the southern gate of the clearing, realizing that a single dead end would be it for us.

Within a few scant steps, I heard the succession of heavy arrows landing behind us.

"*Eyaaargh!*" I shouted, somewhere between a scream and a roar, and ran like the wind. Depending on the angle, some of the fences along the path hid us, but when we had no choice but to expose ourselves in an intersection, for example, a hail of projectiles soon followed.

"How many arrows does he have?!" I ranted. Fortunately, Eugeo was there to tell me the answer.

"That volley just now put him over thirty. It's incredible!"

"Come on, this isn't some lazy MMO...Er, sorry! Forget I said that!"

I'd completely lost all sense of direction by now. But for some reason, at every fork in the path, that tugging sensation at my hairline started up, guiding me either left or right as I ran. So far I was staying ahead of the dragon, but if we got stuck in a single dead end...

Almost as if prompted by my pessimism, I turned left at yet another intersection and found that my mysterious protection had run out. About thirty feet ahead, the path simply ended.

My only option was to use the half-length of chain on my arm to break down the metal fence, but according to the check I did earlier, these fences were close in priority to the chain—they might not go down in one swing.

There wasn't another option at this point, though. I summoned my courage, left my fate up to God, and swung back my arm.

"No, thisaway!"

A voice came out of nowhere, momentarily stopping my brain in its tracks. *Thisaway* was rather folksy, old-fashioned terminology, but the voice was that of a young girl.

I slowed down, looking around, and noticed that just ahead and to the right was a small door I hadn't seen before. Peering out and beckoning us over was a girl, who was indeed maybe ten years old, wearing a black hat.

The round glasses on her nose flashed, and she disappeared through the door. For a moment, I wondered if it was a trap. Then my bangs tugged me onward harder than ever before. It was as if they were saying, *What are you doing? Get in there!*

Eugeo and I raced toward the darkness within that door.

3

The space beyond was much larger and deeper than I had expected.

"Aaaah!"

I wailed as I suddenly did three forward flips through empty air, then landed on my back on a fairly resilient surface. My body bounced, and I landed on my butt a second time.

A moment later, Eugeo landed next to me in a similar manner. We both shook our heads to clear the internal cobwebs, and once my sense of equilibrium had returned, I looked at our surroundings.

"...Huh?" Eugeo mumbled. I couldn't blame him. We'd just leaped through a gate in the middle of the rose garden, so we should have still been in the garden on the other side of it.

But now we were sitting in a hallway, with aged-wood walls, ceiling, and floor. The bounciness of my landing was thanks to the wood. If I'd landed on the paving stones of the garden, I would have lost some life on impact.

The corridor continued a fair ways onward, with a warm orange light flickering at the far end. Even the air had turned from the chilly, damp night to the dry tang of aging paper.

Where are we? I wondered. Then I heard the sound of clinking metal from behind me, far above. I turned around to see a very steep staircase right behind us and, near the top, a small door and smaller person.

I wearily climbed to my feet, the pain in my whipped chest and pierced foot briefly forgotten as I carefully ascended the wooden stairs. The door up there had been bronze fence when we passed through it, but now it was the same wooden material as the rest of the hall. Except that, unlike the antique style of the wood in the hallway, the door itself stood out as looking completely fresh and new.

Once I was three steps from the top, the figure facing the door held out a hand and stopped me. There was a very large cast-iron key ring in her hand, which she had apparently just removed from the door's lock. That clink of metal had been her locking the door, then.

"...Excuse me..."

Where are we? Who are you? I was going to ask, when I noticed a sound. Just beyond the closed door, I heard what made me think of a small, tough creature scratching and scuttling back and forth. I felt the hair on my forearms stand.

"...We've been detected. So much for this back door," the mysterious person muttered, and waved me off again. I had to give up on my questions and descend the stairs again. When I returned to stand next to Eugeo, the person was just coming down behind me.

There were no lights in the hallway, nothing but the faint illumination seeping through from the far end of the hall, so I could make out only a silhouette. She had on a large, bulky hat and a robe like the sort a magician would wear draped around her small body. The keys were in her right hand and a staff taller than she in the left.

That magic staff swung forward, pushing us onward.

"Go on, get down there! Gotta delete this entire hallway now."

The voice was still unmistakably that of a young girl, but for some reason, there was an authority even greater than Miss Azurica's there, and we found ourselves marching quickly toward the light without an argument. At the end of the short hallway, we found ourselves in an extremely strange space.

It was an enormous square chamber, with a number of wall sconces providing warm-toned light. There were no other fixtures but a thick wooden door on the far wall, straight ahead.

On the other three walls were a dozen or more hallways, just like the one we came from. I peered down the one next to ours and saw a dead end, stairs, and a little door.

While Eugeo and I looked around curiously, the robed girl followed us out of the hall, then turned back to face it and raised her staff.

"Hoy!"

She swung the staff with a cute little shout that also sounded like something an old man would say. Nothing should have surprised us at this point, but each successive phenomenon left us stunned. From the far end of the tunnel, the boards on the side walls yanked free one after the other, reassembling as the ground rumbled.

Within a few seconds, the thirty-foot hallway was completely covered, and when the last boards finished placing themselves, it was just a smooth wall. There wasn't a single bit of evidence that there had ever been a hallway behind it.

For sacred arts, this was quite an elaborate, advanced spell. To manipulate a volume of objects that high, you'd need a very long chant and very high System Access Authority. And yet, this strange little girl did all that with a simple "Hoy!" She hadn't even announced a system call first. At the academy, they taught us that every single sacred art required that to initiate.

"Hmph," she snorted, tapping the base of the staff into the ground matter-of-factly, then turning to us at last.

Seen in proper light, she was as cute as a little doll. The black robe shone like velvet and the large hat made of the same material made her look more like an elderly scholar than a magician, but the chestnut-brown curls of hair and milk-white skin under the brim of her hat were youthful.

Most striking of all were her eyes. Behind the round glasses perched on her nose and framed by her long eyelashes were brown eyes the same color as her hair and somehow full of an overwhelming intelligence and wisdom. Looking into them, I felt like I was gazing into an unfathomable depth. There was no way to tell what she was thinking.

But whoever she was, she'd saved us from the Integrity Knight's attack, so I bowed my head to her. "Um…thank you for rescuing us."

"Don't know if it was worth the trouble yet," she muttered, all business. Based on ample experience over our travels, Eugeo was the better choice to negotiate with strangers, so I elbowed him and motioned up front.

He obediently stepped forward and bowed, hair still dripping, and said, "Um…it's nice to meet you. I'm Eugeo, and this is Kirito. Thank you so much for saving us. Um, do you…live here?"

He was clearly disoriented as well. The girl looked annoyed and pushed her glasses up the bridge of her nose. "Of course I don't *live* here…Come."

She cracked the staff against the stone, then started walking toward the large door on the far wall. We hurried after her, watched as she waved the staff to remotely open the door—and received yet another shock.

When we passed through the door after her and found ourselves in another mysterious new space, all we could do was stare.

It was a stunning sight. The only way to describe it in one phrase was "a gigantic library."

A world of infinite shelves and books. It was circular as a whole but with numerous staircases and walkways along the walls, which were lined on one or both sides with massive bookshelves. The span from the floor to the ceiling over the maze of shelves was tall enough to fit a ten-story building inside. I couldn't even imagine the total number of books contained in all these shelves.

There was no way a structure large enough to house this library could be in the rose garden. I gazed up at the gloomy ceiling far above and asked, "Is…is this inside the Central Cathedral?"

"You could say that. And you could say it's not," the girl said. I thought I detected a note of satisfaction in her voice. "Because I removed its original door, this great library exists within the cathedral, but none can enter—without my invitation."

"Great…library…?" Eugeo mumbled, looking around in disbelief.

"Aye. This library contains all historical records dating back to the creation of this world, the formulas that govern its every working function, and all the system commands that you call sacred arts."

…System commands?!

I couldn't believe the words I was hearing at first. I stared at the girl, and through half-open lips, I heard my own voice say, "Wh-who…*are*…you?"

She looked at me, clearly understanding the shock I had received and the reason for it, and introduced herself.

"My name is Cardinal. I was once the coordinator of this world, but now I am merely the sole librarian of this facility."

Cardinal.

To me, that word held three meanings.

First was the senior rank in the Catholic Church of the real world.

Second was the name of a bird, so named because its plumage was the same vivid red as the robes worn by the aforementioned priests.

And third was from "Cardinal System," the highly advanced autonomous program that Akihiko Kayaba developed to run his VRMMO game. The original version was utilized in *SAO*, where it held the players in the palm of its hand, fine-tuning the economy, items, and monster generation to exacting effect.

After we beat *SAO*, Kayaba fried his brain by scanning it with a prototype STL, but before doing so, he created a bite-size version of the Cardinal System and included it in a suite of VRMMO development tools called The Seed.

The thought-simulation program Kayaba left behind in cyberspace helped The Seed spread throughout the Net, where it controlled many other games such as *Gun Gale Online*. I had a part in The Seed's free distribution, and for a long time, I'd wondered what Kayaba's true goals were, but I had never come to a satisfying answer. Knowing him, there was no way he'd release his dev kit for free just to absolve his sins in creating the *SAO* Incident...

That all aside, could this girl here be a personification of that very same Cardinal System?

It was possible, of course, that within the Axiom Church there was a senior rank that they named after the real-life cardinal. But she mentioned that she was once the "coordinator" of the world. Not the leader, not the ruler: Cardinal the Coordinator.

But why would the Cardinal System be here? Was the Underworld built using The Seed? And if that were the case, why would the coordination system, the "invisible hand of God," take human form? Unlike with Yui, the counseling program, the Cardinal System wasn't supposed to be able to talk with players, I thought.

I was totally paralyzed with questions, and Eugeo seemed fairly stunned himself. He managed to mumble, "All...of history...? You mean an entire chronology from the founding of the four empires to now? Here...?"

"And not only that. There's even a record of the Creation, when Stacia and Vecta split the world between the human empire and the Dark Territory."

He swayed back and forth, looking ready to pass out—Eugeo was a history buff. The mysterious girl named Cardinal pushed her glasses up again and grinned mischievously. "What do you say? My stories can run a lil' long, so why don't you have a meal and a rest first? If you want to read, all the books are open to you. However many you want, for as long as you want."

She swung her staff with another "Hoy!" and a small, round

table simply pushed its way up out of the floor next to her. It was piled high with steaming food—sandwiches, meat buns, sausages, fried pastries.

The sight prompted immediate pangs in my stomach after a night of sipping water and nibbling on hard bread, but Eugeo seemed to feel guilty about chowing down and reading books while we were on our mission to rescue Alice. He looked to me with misgivings plain on his face, so I had to shrug and explain. "We had enough trouble against Eldrie, and there's no way we can push through against an archer knight on his dragon. Let's rest, recuperate, and work on a new plan. It seems safe here, and we've lost a lot of life already."

"Indeed. I've placed a charm so that if you eat, your wounds will heal. But first, hold out your right hands," the girl commanded. We did as she said, holding out the arms that still bore the shackles. With two waves of her staff, the heavy rings split apart and fell to the floor.

We rubbed our bare wrists, freed for the first time in two days. Eugeo still looked conflicted, but then he scrunched up his face and sneezed. He'd fallen headfirst into the fountain during the fight with Eldrie and was still soaking wet. If we didn't get that addressed, he'd wind up with a "Head Cold" negative status effect.

"You seem like you could use a good warm-up before you eat," the girl said. "At the end of that hall there, you'll find a small bath. You can eat and read after that."

I didn't think we were going to end up sleeping here, but Eugeo did at least seem to accept her offer.

"...Thank you. I'll do that, C-Cardinal. Um, and...where would that record of the Creation be?"

Cardinal lifted her staff and pointed toward a particularly large cluster of shelves situated quite high up in the library.

"From that staircase upward is the history wing."

"Thank you! Well...I'll be off now."

He bowed again, sneezed again, then disappeared down the

narrow path between the bookcases. Cardinal watched him go, then muttered, "Sadly, the record of Creation here is an artificial one, dictated by the Axiom Church's pontifex to a scribe."

I leaned over toward the girl's hat and asked quietly, "So…are the gods of this world a fiction? No Stacia, no Solus, no Terraria…no Vecta?"

"None," Cardinal said simply. "The religious myths the people of the Underworld believe are merely stories spread by the Church to maintain its stranglehold. The gods' names are registered as supervisor accounts in case of emergencies, but the people outside have never once logged in using them."

That answer cleared up a portion of my questions, at least. I stared into those burnt-brown eyes and said, "You're not an Underworldian, though. You're more like an outsider…like the system admins."

"Indeed. And so are you, Kirito the Unregistered."

"…Yeah. So am I."

At long last, after two years and two months, I had unshakable certainty that this was not some alternate dimension but a virtual world created by human beings in base reality. I felt a powerful sensation rising, taking me by surprise. I sucked in a deep breath and exhaled. There were so many things to ask that I didn't know where to start. But there was one thing I had to confirm.

"The name of the ones who created the Underworld is Rath, R-A-T-H. Correct?"

"Indeed."

"And you are the Cardinal System, the autonomous program that operates and manages the virtual world."

As soon as I said this, the girl's eyes widened. "Ahh, you know about me? Have you interacted with my kind on the other side?"

"…Er, sure."

Interaction didn't cover the half of it. I spent two years in Aincrad fighting for my life, and the greatest enemy of all, in a way, was the Cardinal System. I didn't think that would make much sense to her, though.

"But…as far as I knew, the Cardinal System never had a personified interface like you. So…what does that make you? What do you do here?"

Cardinal smiled faintly at the succession of questions. She pushed a curly lock of hair from her forehead back under her cap and, in that strange voice that was both young and old, said, "It will be…a very, very long story. Why did I isolate myself in this library…? Why did I wait to make contact with you…? It is a very long story indeed…"

She paused, appearing to lose herself in reminiscence, then looked up. "I can sum it up as quickly as I can. But first, eat. Your wounds must be plaguing you."

The succession of wild experiences had pushed the pain to the back of my mind, but as soon as she pointed it out, I felt an instant throb in my chest where Eldrie had whipped me and in my right foot where the knight had shot me.

On her instructions, I grabbed a piping-hot steamed bun from the table and took a hearty bite. The meat was every bit as delicious as the stuff in the buns I slipped out of school to buy from Gottoro's in town. Enraptured, I continued stuffing it into my face. Whatever commands she had put on the food, each bite caused the pain to dim and the wounds to close up and heal.

"Just like a true admin…you can adjust the food settings to anything you want," I marveled.

Cardinal snorted and said, "Two mistakes. I'm not an administrator. And I can only manipulate objects within this library."

She turned away and started walking down the aisle along the curved wall. I picked up all the buns and sandwiches I could carry and cast a glance at the hallway toward the bath. He'd need a good long soak to avoid getting a cold, so Eugeo wouldn't be emerging anytime soon…

"…Hmm? Wait…if you can heal wounds with food, shouldn't

it protect against sickness, too?" I pointed out. Cardinal looked back and grinned. Apparently the bath was just an excuse to get Eugeo away from us.

I followed the scheming sage down the library path, through fork after fork, ascending and descending, until I no longer had any idea where in the library we were. Just as I was finishing up my meal of magical food—eating while walking, a major breach of etiquette—we came to a circular space surrounded entirely by shelves. There was a table in the middle and two old-fashioned chairs.

Cardinal plopped herself down on one of the chairs and pointed at the other with her staff. I obediently sat down.

Instantly, there were two cups of tea on the tabletop. Cardinal lifted her mug, took a sip, and said, "Have you ever wondered why it is that this peaceful, artificial world contains a feudal system?"

It took me a few seconds to remember the unfamiliar word. Feudalism—the social system whereby local landowners were effectively nobles who had complete control over their territory. It was the system of the Middle Ages, with emperors, kings, barons, dukes, and the like, and so common in fantasy-themed books and games that the few exceptions were notable in their own right.

The Underworld fit right into that medieval European mold, so it seemed perfectly natural to me that it had its own nobles and emperors and such. Cardinal's question took me by surprise.

"Uh...why...? Isn't it because the realm's designers set it up that way?"

"Not so," Cardinal said, her mouth upturned with the anticipation that I would have responded that way. "The outside people who created this world merely set down the vessel. The social structure you see here was created entirely by the Underworldians who live here."

"I see..."

It made sense that we were excluding Eugeo from this conversation. At last, I recalled one of the first things I wanted to clear up with her. She'd demonstrated familiarity with Rath. So did that mean…?

"H-hang on. Can you make contact with the real world? Is there some method of relaying information?" I asked with excitement.

She looked annoyed. "Fool. If I could do that, I wouldn't have locked myself up in this dusty place for centuries. The only one who can do that…is the pontifex."

"Oh…I see…"

That made me even more curious about the figure in question, but I set that aside and clung to my one ray of hope. "Then, can you tell what date it is in the real world…or where my physical body is located, or—"

"I'm afraid I can't access the system domain now. Even my ability to browse the data register is meager. Compared to the Cardinal you knew on the other side, I am a helpless creation," she said bashfully, making a disappointed face that suited her apparent age. I almost began to feel a bit sorry for her.

"No," I said, shaking my head, "it's a huge help that you even know about the real world at all. Sorry to have derailed your explanation…you were talking about feudalism." I gave the topic a bit of thought and guessed, "Does it have something to do with…needing a manager in place to maintain security or distribute goods?"

"But as you know by now, the people of this world do not disobey the law as a fundamental rule. They do not harm others, steal, or monopolize harvests. But if their diligence and fairness were enforced by nature, you would assume they'd form a more effective social development, like communism. Do you think such people, in a world of barely a hundred thousand, really need four emperors and various ranks of nobles numbering over a thousand?"

"A hundred…"

I hadn't heard the total population of the Underworld yet. Cardinal said "barely," but I was stunned at the total. This wasn't artificial-intelligence research, it was a full-scale simulation of an entire civilization.

But as she said, each emperor ruling over twenty-five thousand subjects seemed quite small when compared to the Roman Empire or the Frankish Kingdom. It didn't seem like a feudalism that arose out of need but one built to mimic the real-life example.

As I pored this over, Cardinal again offered some fundamental truths.

"Earlier I said that there were no gods in this world. But in the age of Creation—four hundred and fifty years ago—there were those who resembled that title. Four 'gods'…back when Centoria was just a tiny village."

"Four hundred and fifty? Not three hundred and eighty? I mean, it's the year—" I started to say, but she shrugged in exasperation.

"What did I tell you? The Church invented the creation myth. The genesis of the current calendar was arbitrarily decided afterward."

"Uh…Oh. So, four gods, you said? Those were humans…staffers of Rath who built this world, right?"

This time, Cardinal grinned, telling me that I was on the right track. "So you can deduce that much?"

"In this world, the chicken would have come before the egg. Someone had to raise the first artificial fluctlights from babies. Otherwise it wouldn't make sense that all these people are speaking and writing in Japanese."

"Very wisely argued. You are indeed correct. In the beginning, when I was still a manager without sentience, four outsiders descended upon this land, separated into two farms, and raised eight children each. They taught them how to read and write, to raise crops, to tend to livestock…even the moral arguments of good and evil that anchored the Taboo Index later on."

"So they really were gods. That's a lot of responsibility…even a single offhand comment could end up having a huge impact on the outcome of the entire society."

Cardinal nodded gravely. "Indeed. It was only after I was

imprisoned inside this library that I was able to collect these thoughts and come to one conclusion—why does this world feature an unnecessary feudalism? Why does it have such an extreme legal system, and why do some nobles sneak through its cracks for their own profit and pleasure? There could be only one answer."

She pushed up her round little glasses and intoned, "Given that the Four Progenitors succeeded at their extremely difficult task, it is clear that they possessed the highest intelligence that a human being can have. And given the moral sense of good they instilled in the Underworldians, their good moral character is apparent as well—except that this did not apply to all four of them."

"…What…?"

"While all four were brilliant, one of them was not possessed of a good heart. And that one was the source of *pollution* that infected one or two of those first children. I doubt that it was by design…but one's nature cannot be hidden. That source introduced self-interested desires, like possessiveness and dominance. And that child, or children, became the founder of what developed into the nobles, emperors, and high priests of the Axiom Church that control this world now…"

Not possessed…of a good heart?

So that evilness that dwelt in a certain subsection of nobles originally came from one of the core members of Rath? And the evil was passed down mentally, until it ultimately resulted in people like Raios Antinous and Humbert Zizek today?

I suddenly felt my senses grow distant and cold. In the real world, my unconscious body was connected to an STL in Rath's headquarters, wherever that was. The thought that right near me was the person responsible for Raios gave me the chills.

Was it someone I knew? I tried to remember the faces of the Rath staffers, but the only ones that appeared immediately were Takeru Higa, the chief researcher, and the mysterious public servant Seijirou Kikuoka, who got me in with Rath. There were other employees at the branch office in Roppongi, of course, but my memory of their names and faces was vague. In my perceived time, that little job for Rath was over two years ago.

The question was, did this just happen to be a person who was greedy and self-interested, or was it someone who infiltrated Rath with sinister designs? Someone stealing secrets, selling them…possibly destroying them?

"Cardinal…do you know the names of these Four Progenitors?" I asked. She shook her head sadly.

"I would need access to the entire system domain to know that."

"Oh…sorry. I don't mean to keep asking you the same things."

It wasn't like knowing the names was going to help me now. It merely made the need to create contact with the other side that much more crucial. I leaned back against the chair, sipped the sweet-smelling tea, and changed the subject.

"I see…So if a small subset of Underworldians possesses this sense of dominance, then it's a natural evolution that they would develop into a privileged class. They're like lions among a herd of gazelles."

"And like a virus that cannot be deleted. In this world, children do not just inherit physical appearance but mentality as well. Among the lower nobles, where marriage with commoners happens more often, that self-interest seems much weaker…"

Her words put me in mind of Ronie and Tiese, sixth-rank nobles who possessed a very respectable sense of justice and benevolence.

"Meaning…that if the nobles marry among one another, their self-interest is preserved?"

"Quite. The four imperial dynasties and the Church's high priests are the backbone of this. And standing atop them all is the ultimate ruler of the human empire…the Axiom Church's pontifex, and now a system administrator. In fact, she has taken that haughty title for her own name: Administrator."

"Adminis…trator," I muttered, repeating the English term. Now that she said it, I recalled Eldrie babbling that name when his forehead starting glowing. So that meant the target of the Integrity Knights' fealty was the Administrator Pontifex...

That was when I stumbled over another very important bit of information in Cardinal's statement. "Wait...did you say *she*? This...pontifex?"

Ever since I became familiar with it, I had just assumed that the leader of the Axiom Church would be an elderly man, but it seemed I was wrong.

Cardinal nodded and scowled like never before. "Exactly. And worst of all...you might say she is my twin sister."

"Wh-what do you mean?" I asked, unable to parse the logic of that, but the sage in the guise of a young girl did not answer quickly. She looked at her own pale, fragile hand in apparent disgust, and only then opened her mouth to speak.

"I will tell you in order...About three hundred and fifty years ago, the Axiom Church was founded to serve as the supreme controlling structure of society. In other words, about a hundred years after the simulation actually began. At the time, all humans married around age twenty and had an average of five children, so the population was over six hundred in the fifth generation alone, and near a thousand if you counted their parents and grandparents..."

"H-hang on. How do marriage and childbirth even work in this world?" I asked, unable to resist getting answers to questions I'd had for two whole years, and then panicked when the question seemed a bit inappropriate for a girl of around ten—regardless of who she was on the inside.

But Cardinal didn't bat an eye. She said, "I do not know the breeding habits of real-world human beings, so I cannot say for certain, but I believe that the act itself is largely based on the real thing, given the fundamental structure of the fluctlight. When a man and woman registered as spouses by the system—and they alone—commit the act, there is a certain probability that the woman will become with child. In more direct terms, a new fluctlight prototype is loaded into an empty cube in the Lightcube Cluster, synthesized between his parents' physical attributes and mental/personality patterns, and then activated as a newborn baby."

"Ah, I see...And what's this marriage registration?"

"Just a simple system command, delivered as an oath of marriage dedicated to Stacia. The village elder did it in the early days, but once churches started popping up around the place, the monks and nuns would officiate."

"Ahhh...Oops, sorry to interrupt again. Please continue," I prompted. She nodded and went on.

"Several decades after the Four Progenitors logged out, there were a thousand residents, already ruled by a number of lords. Those few who had received the weapon of self-interest grew their territory as far as they could, and when the young people nearby could not manage their own fields anymore, they were put to use as serfs. Some resisted the yoke and chose to leave the center of the map for new frontiers."

"Okay, so those were the people who ended up starting rural towns like Zakkaria and Rulid."

"Precisely. The lords in control of the center were antagonistic to one another, of course, so they did not join their houses in marriage for quite a while. Eventually, two lords conspired to wed their families together...and produced a child. She was as cute as an angel and possessed the greatest self-interest of any fluctlight created in the Underworld...They called her Quinella."

Cardinal stared out into space, her eyes glimmering as though traveling the long-distant past.

The lamps placed between the bookshelves surrounding this little room cast complex shadows on her white cheeks. You could have heard a pin drop in the silence. When she spoke again, her voice was calm but had a note of melancholy.

"In Centoria at the time—which had grown into a full town, not just a village—it was one of the lords, Quinella's father, who assigned children their callings. By the time she turned ten, she showed great talent for the sword, sacred arts, singing, weaving, and every other activity, so everyone assumed that she could shine at any calling he might give her. But because of that, Quinella's father decided he didn't want to send his precious daughter out to work..."

A pitying smile crept over her features. "It was a foolish fixation. In order to keep Quinella close to him, he gave his daughter a calling that had never existed before: training in sacred arts. In a room in the back of their mansion, Quinella used all her wits to analyze the sacred arts—which are really system commands. Before then, the Underworldians knew only the most basic of commands, and none even bothered to question the meaning of the words themselves. They hadn't needed to, in order to live their lives."

Thinking back to my time in Rulid Village, the most that Eugeo and the other villagers did was open Stacia Windows to check remaining life.

"But with tremendous patience and observation for a child her age, Quinella continued to analyze the command words— strange, otherworldly terms from a language not their own, like *generate* and *element* and *object*. Finally, she succeeded in creating her own art based on a few basic commands: Thermal Arrow. From the system commands that were merely tools to assist one's living, she had created an attack spell that would harm the life of its target...Kirito."

The sound of my name snapped me out of my reverie. I looked back at her.

"Do you know why your sacred arts usage level—your System Access Authority—rose so abruptly before?"

"Yeah. Well, I think so. It was because we beat those monsters... the goblin pack in the cave."

"Precisely. This world was originally designed for the residents to fight invading enemies from outside and increase in strength. That will become necessary during the 'stress test stage'...But at any rate, to raise one's authority level requires defeating an invader or simple repetition of commands. At the mere age of eleven, Quinella discovered how to do that all on her own. She went into the woods near her home and used that Thermal Arrow on the harmless golden flying foxes…"

"Meaning…that the target you can defeat to raise your authority isn't just limited to invaders like monsters from the Dark Territory…?"

"Aye. In other words, the accumulation of experience points occurs when any moving unit is destroyed, including humans. Of course, humans do not kill humans in this world, and almost no human would kill a harmless animal—but those with a high amount of noble genes are a different story. They hunt for sport and, without realizing it, increase their authority level…and it was eleven-year-old Quinella who did this while knowing her own intentions."

Cardinal paused there and quietly put the cup to her lips. She pulled it away and cradled it in her hands before continuing.

"When she realized that she could raise her sacred arts usage level by killing animals, she started sneaking into the forest at night to kill without alerting her family or the villagers. As the process in charge of world balance at the time, if I'd been conscious, Quinella's actions would have terrified me. Without emotion…or perhaps with a kind of joy, she cleaned out all the wild animal units around Centoria in a single night. As the system ordained, the depleted unit numbers were replenished…and then she repeated the act the next night…"

To a VRMMO gamer like me, that was a totally ordinary action. In the *SAO* days, I did that very thing myself, hunting for days at a time for the sole purpose of increasing my own stats. It was the entire point of an MMO.

But hearing the words from Cardinal made a cold sweat run down my back. A young girl in pajamas, prowling the forest at night and burning any animal she found, without emotion. If anything, that was the image of a nightmare.

As though resonating with my own fear, Cardinal's hands squeezed the cup tighter.

"Quinella's authority level rose without end. Her decoding of commands proceeded until she could use arts that the people of the time would have considered miracles, like life regeneration and weather prediction. Her father and the other residents of Centoria called her the child of God and began to worship her. At age thirteen, her beauty had indeed become divine. Behind her gentle smile, Quinella sensed that the time had come to satisfy her bottomless lust for power. She wanted not the power of land possession like the feudal lords, nor the strength of the warriors and their swords…but a more absolute form of power…using the name of God…"

For a brief moment, Cardinal looked up to the dome of the Great Library, hanging far overhead, or perhaps to the real world beyond even that.

"It was the greatest mistake of those who built this world that they described the mysterious powers of its system commands through the concept of God. In my mind…the existence of God is an irresistible ambrosia to the human mind. It can heal all ills and permit all cruelties. Fortunately, as I do not possess emotions, I cannot hear His voice…"

Her burnt-brown eyes looked down on the teacup, and she tapped its ceramic rim with a finger. More hot liquid began to fill in from the base, until the empty cup was full of fresh tea again.

"You need not be a blind believer when miracles are performed before your eyes and explained as the work of a god. Men injured on the farm, healed in a snap. Storms foretold three days before their arrival. No one doubted Quinella's word ever again. She told the lords working under her father that they needed a place of worship, to call forth ever greater miracles. Very soon, they had built a marble tower in the middle of the village. It was narrow back then, and only three stories tall…but that was the foundation of this very Central Cathedral and the founding of the Axiom Church's three hundred and fifty years of history."

The story of this ancient saint, Quinella, put me in mind of a different person. I'd never known her myself, only through

Eugeo's and Selka's stories—but the girl Cardinal described sounded a lot like the girl with the talent for sacred arts at a young age, tasked with being an apprentice sister at the church: Alice Zuberg.

But Eugeo claimed that when she was in Rulid, Alice was kind and warm to everyone. And she was Selka's sister, too. I couldn't imagine such a person would sneak out at night to lay waste to wild animals.

So how had Alice increased her System Access Authority? I started sinking into the quagmire of that question when Cardinal's voice brought me back.

"At the time, the people believed, without exception, that Quinella was a priestess blessed by Stacia herself. They prayed at the tower morning and night and gladly gave up a portion of their harvests. At first, those lords who weren't her blood relatives did not think kindly of her...but Quinella was a hardy soul. She gave all the landowners noble titles in God's name. Until that point, some of the farmers were unhappy about donating a portion of their harvests to their feudal lords, but once that became a divine right, they had no choice but to obey. Now that they were proper nobility, the feudal lords decided that it was in their best interests to follow Quinella rather than oppose her."

She set the teacup down on its saucer, the hard surface clinking, then stared me right in the eyes. "It was longer than I intended, but that is the story of why feudalism exists in the Underworld."

"I see. So it wasn't a system that arose to maintain society out of necessity but in order to rule it...I suppose that would explain why the higher nobles don't feel responsibility toward the realm," I muttered.

Cardinal grimaced and said, "I doubt you have seen it for yourself, but the actions of the great nobles and imperial families on their own territory are truly awful. If the Taboo Index did not forbid murder and assault, I cannot imagine the carnage that would unfold there."

"...And was it Quinella who created the Taboo Index, too?

Does that mean that she did have some kind of moral compass after all?"

"Hah! I wouldn't say that," Cardinal said, snorting adorably. "Even after long years of thought, I still do not know the reason that the people of this world cannot break the rules imposed by their social superiors. Even I am not an exception. Although the Axiom Church does not rule over me, and thus the Taboo Index does not bind me…I must still obey a number of rules created for the Cardinal program. The fact that I have been locked in this place for centuries should tell you that I am shackled by an inescapable fate."

"Is Quinella bound by higher rules still, too?"

"Of course. Because she created the Taboo Index, that preposterous set of laws does not apply to her…but she still could not break the rules set by her parents when she was young, and now she is controlled by new orders. Think—if her parents had not commanded, 'you must not harm people,' would she have been satisfied just killing animals? Of course she would kill humans. The authority level gain would have been higher."

Again I felt a prickle run along my back. I tried to ignore the sensation and said, "Okay…so in this world, the concept of not hurting people was one of the very first taboos, those lessons that the Four Progenitors instilled in their children. And Quinella put that into writing and added a more complex system and series of rules to it?"

"In appearance only. But it was not out of any wish for the world to be peaceful. When she was in her mid-twenties, Quinella was even more beautiful, the tower was even taller, and she had many disciples doing her bidding. Similar white towers appeared in other villages, and under the official name of the Axiom Church, Quinella's rule was becoming ironclad. But as the population grew, along with the expansion of human settlements, Quinella became concerned about the places beyond her sight. She was worried that others in the more distant reaches of the land might discover the secret of one's sacred arts level, as she did. So she decided to stipulate laws that would ensure she had control over all human beings. The first law was absolute loyalty to the Axiom Church, and the second law was against the act of murder. Why do you suppose she did that?"

She paused and stared at me. I waited for the answer.

"Because killing humans would raise one's authority level. That is the only reason the Church outlawed murder. There is no virtue, no morality, no sense of goodness or justice behind it."

Stunned, I couldn't help but argue back. "B-but...didn't the Four Progenitors instill a moral taboo against murder and harm from the beginning? Didn't the people have those values already, before the Church told them so?"

"And what if that lesson must come from the parent? What about the slim chance that after birth, a child could be separated from its parent—its first higher structure—and end up growing without that moral education? If such a child had the noble genes, it might kill people around it in its greed and gain an authority level higher than Quinella's. So in order to minimize that possibility, she put together a book called the Taboo Index and placed it in every town and village. Parents were obligated to teach the entire Taboo Index to their children from page one, as soon as they were old enough to understand language. You see? If the people of this world seem to be overly good, diligent, and benevolent, it is because having them that way suits the purposes of the structure that controls them."

"B-but..."

I kept shaking my head, unwilling to take Cardinal's explanation at face value. All those people I'd met in Rulid, along the trip, and at the Swordcraft Academy—Selka, Ronie, Tiese, Sortiliena, and, most of all, Eugeo—couldn't have been as warm and human as they were because the program *forced* them to be.

"But...that's not *all* there is to it, right? Isn't there...something in the fluctlight archetype as well? Something that's placed in our human souls from the very start..."

"You have seen the evidence against that argument for yourself already," Cardinal said. I stopped in my tracks, taken aback.

"Huh…?"

"Think of the goblins who attempted to kill you and Eugeo for sport. You didn't really think of them as programmed code, either, did you? They are what happens to the fluctlight archetype when it is given orders that are the antithesis of the Taboo Index—kill, steal, live by your desires. You see, they are 'people,' too, just as much as you are."

"Ah…"

I had nothing to say to that.

I'd had a suspicion this was the case. Just over two years ago, when I saw and heard the mannerisms of those goblins I fought beneath the End Mountains, I felt that they were far too natural to be those programmed NPCs or monsters from a typical VRMMO. The look of greed in those yellow eyes was subtler than any simple texture mapping could re-create.

But that just made it harder to shrug off the knowledge that they were human beings with proper fluctlights. I killed two of those goblins to save Eugeo and Selka, but they were just following the greed etched into their souls. Eugeo had surpassed the limitations of the Taboo Index, so surely goblins could also potentially turn away from their orders to kill and steal. Yet I assumed, just because they were goblins and they looked scary, that they must therefore be evil, and I unleashed my sword upon them without another thought…

"Don't think too hard, fool," Cardinal scolded. "Are you imagining yourself to be a god now? You can ponder it for a century or two and still won't find any answers. Even now, as I've finally come across someone like you, I am conflicted…"

She looked up, brows knitted, then stared into her cup. When she spoke again, there was a poetic cast to her words.

"Once, I was a manager without hesitation or qualm. I moved the world by unshakable principles, sparing not a thought for the tiny things in the palm of my hand. But now, in human form…I finally know the fixation on life…I doubt that those who created this world truly understand what it is they have brought about.

For they are gods, too…If they learn of Quinella's atrocities, they might be interested but never mournful. When this world enters the stress test stage, it is inevitable that this will all descend into a hell too horrific to describe—"

"Oh…that! What is this stress test you keep mentioning…?" I interrupted.

Cardinal glanced up again and bobbed her head. "Yes, I should get back to the topic. Let's go in order—I was explaining that Quinella had distributed the Taboo Index throughout the world. That text solidified the Axiom Church's control. By adding more and more entries to the index, Quinella not only sharpened the moral compass of the populace to better suit the Church's needs, she also eliminated the various issues that threatened the people's livelihoods. It forbid wandering into swamps labeled sources of infectious diseases, identified grasses that prevented the flow of milk in goats that ate them, and so on…As long as they unthinkingly followed the text, no problems would ever arise. Over the years, the people put their blind faith into the Church, until not a single person ever doubted its first rule: Thou must obey the Church."

It was total control. An ideal society without starvation, rebellion, or revolution.

"The population of Centoria exploded, and with new, advanced construction techniques using large-scale commands, that little village grew into a splendid city. The Axiom Church's property grew to the size you see now, and the tower only grew taller…If anything symbolized Quinella's endless desire, it was this tower. She did not know what it meant to be sated. As she turned thirty, then forty, and her beauty faded, it only got worse. It was not the kind of base gluttony of the nobles, with their hedonistic pleasures. After a time, Quinella no longer walked on the surface but stayed locked within the top floor of the ever-growing tower, deciphering more and more of the world's sacred arts. She sought further authority, greater secrets…until at last, she surpassed the final, ultimate barrier of all: her life."

The statistic known as "life" was represented in an exceedingly clear way. It grew along with the user's life span, peaking around the twenties or thirties, then slowly descended until it reached zero somewhere between age sixty and eighty. My life had grown quite a bit in the last two years. Seeing it dwindle a bit each day had to be terrifying—especially to a conqueror who had the entire world in her grasp.

"But…no matter how many commands she deciphered and skills she mastered—including even the weather—the limit of her life itself, her natural life span, was an irrefutable fact. Only those with administrative status could alter it—such as an outside admin or the autonomous control program, Cardinal. Quinella's life sank, day after day. She turned fifty, then sixty…There was no longer a shred of the beauty that had enraptured so many. Walking became impossible. She was confined to her luxurious bed in the room that overlooked the rest of the world. Once an hour, she would examine her Stacia Window, confirming the numbers as they dropped…"

Cardinal paused. She wrapped her hands around her small body as if to ward off a chill.

"But even then, Quinella did not give up. Her tenacity was tremendous…With her cracked and faded voice, she continued testing all combinations of sounds, trying to call forth that forbidden command. These vain efforts should not have succeeded. The odds would be like flipping a coin that lands heads up a thousand times in a row…perhaps even less likely than that. But…however…"

I felt a sudden, indescribable shiver come over me. Cardinal—this strange girl who insisted that she was merely a system without emotions—was expressing a kind of fear, in no uncertain terms.

"Finally, she was on the brink of death…One little scratch, a mere brush with illness, and it would have all been over…and on that very night, Quinella finally opened the forbidden door. It was an impossible coincidence—in fact, I even suspect that someone from the outside world might have assisted her. I can show it to you, not that you can use it."

She brandished her staff in her left hand and whispered, "System Call! Inspect Entire Command List!"

And with a tremendously deep and rich sound the likes of which I'd never heard before, a purple window larger than usual opened in front of her.

That was all. No holy light from above, no chorus of angels with trumpets blowing a fanfare. But I understood the tremendous effect of that command.

It was the ultimate sacred art. A thing that should not be.

"I think you've figured it out. Yes, this window contains a list of every system command there is. This was another colossal mistake of the founders of this world. They should have removed this command the very instant the Four Progenitors who needed it finally left this realm."

She swung her staff again, and the forbidden list vanished.

"Quinella pored over the list with fading eyes. Then she understood it all, and rejoiced, and literally stood up and danced. The command she sought was at the end of the list: the command to take over all of the Cardinal System's privileges in case of a world-balance emergency requiring manual control. The command to become a true god…"

Suddenly, the image floated into my brain, vivid and clear.

The top of a tower that reached all the way into the sky. Beyond the windows, a starless night choked with roiling clouds and brilliant flashes of lightning.

In the center of the wide, empty room was a single canopy bed. But its owner was not lying down in it. She stood on the soft mattress, colorless long hair flying to and fro, sagging flesh writhing in a bizarre dance. Her arms jutted from white silk pajamas like dead branches, and her neck curved backward so that a roar of joy could surge from her throat. Against the accompaniment of the intensifying thunder she squawked, like some monstrous bird, the forbidden command to usurp the throne of God…

The Underworld was no longer an AI test, nor some kind of virtual civilization simulator.

The Rath staffers who created this world, like Seijirou Kikuoka and Takeru Higa, had lived for only thirty-something years. But at the time that Quinella, pure dominance incarnate, had gained full administrative status at last, she was already eighty. If Cardinal's story was accurate, she had lived nearly another three hundred years since then. Who could estimate what kind of being such an intellect would be now?

Did Rath really have everything under control? How much did they understand about what was happening here…?

The black-robed young sage and I stared at each other, each grappling with our own fear.

There were no doors in the Great Library—we were completely cut off from the rest of the world. And yet, I thought I heard the low rumble of thunder in the distance.

That ominous sound heralded a new storm along the path that should have been near its end—a storm greater than any we had yet encountered.

(To be continued)

AFTERWORD

Hello, this is Reki Kawahara. Thank you for reading *Sword Art Online 11: Alicization Turning*. I chose this subtitle in the sense of it being a turning point, but as for whether this is materially the midpoint of the Alicization arc...sorry, I can't be sure of that yet! In terms of content, however, it brings an end to Kirito's and Eugeo's school life and shifts the story to a new phase. And then, from a character with a name familiar to Kirito, we learn the secrets of the Underworld's creation...and then, *splat*—run headlong into the end of the book. I have no good excuses for this abrupt finish and will endeavor to bring you the twelfth volume as soon as possible, so please join me there.

This book is the sixth I've had published this year, which means I've somehow managed to maintain my pace of six books a year since my professional debut in 2009. This year of 2012 was a huge one for me, as both *Accel World* and *Sword Art Online* received anime series, and my encounters with people from various walks of life have given me a lot to think about when it comes to my own writing. I don't have the space to explain all that here, but if put in a nutshell, it would be "to take my story creation seriously but enjoy it as well."

Writing books is a personal task, and when you're in your private thoughts, there are times when you get depressed. But enjoying yourself and your process is the basis of creative motivation, so I want to get back to basics and just enjoy each book as I write next year. I hope to continue my six-books-a-year pace as long as I can! I'm not doing this just to rack up streaks, of course, but I know from personal experience that once I fall off a certain pace, I never get back there. So I want to keep alternating *SAO* and *AW* every other month until I finish them...*he said, thus putting more pressure on himself.*

I started the *Progressive* series this year as well, which meant four volumes of *SAO*. I must express my utter thanks to abec, who provided so many wonderful interior illustrations, despite being busy already with the incredible amount of anime work to do. To my editors Mr. Miki and Mr. Tsuchiya, I'm sorry for being late at various stages. Even this afterword is thirty minutes overdue!

And of course, to all of you still following along, my deepest thanks. Hope to see you again next year!

Reki Kawahara—October 2012